Frozen Vengeance

Patricia Fisher Mystery Adventures

Book 6

Steve Higgs

Text Copyright © 2020 Steven J Higgs

Publisher: Steve Higgs

The right of Steve Higgs to be identified as author of the Work has been asserted by him in accordance with the Copyright, Designs and Patents Act 1988

All rights reserved.

The book is copyright material and must not be copied, reproduced, transferred, distributed, leased, licensed or publicly performed or used in any way except as specifically permitted in writing by the publishers, as allowed under the terms and conditions under which it was purchased or as strictly permitted by applicable copyright law. Any unauthorised distribution or use of this text may be a direct infringement of the author's and publisher's rights and those responsible may be liable in law accordingly.

'Frozen Vengeance' is a work of fiction. Names, characters, businesses, organisations, places, events and incidents either are the product of the author's imagination or are used fictitiously. Any resemblance to actual persons, living or dead, events or locations is entirely coincidental.

Dedication

This book is dedicated to Victoria Seymour, a competition winner who gave Patricia Fisher a middle name at long last. You will have to read the next book to find out what it is though.

Victoria gets a signed copy of the book and her name here in the dedication forever.

Table of Contents

Prologue: Wrong Place Wrong Time

Grand Arrival

Settling In

Problems Onboard

Mystery Guest

Royalty

Abandon Ship!

Bowels of the Ship

Baker and Schneider

Sabotage

Missing Molly

Search

Murder Most Unexpected

The Bridge

Uniform

Sombre Moments

Molly Returns

Captive

Breakfast Session

Creepy Steward

What's the Worst They Could Have Planned?

Double Cross

Suicide Note

Need Him Alive!

Unhappy Hero

Picking it Apart

Denial

Terror on the High Seas

Loyalty and Deceit

Lights Out

What Sam Said

Assault the Bridge

Blind Threat

Ambush

Frozen Vengeance

Warming Up

Breakfast

Author's Note

More Books with Patricia Fisher

More Cozy Mystery by Steve Higgs

More Books by Steve Higgs

Free Books and More

Prologue: Wrong Place Wrong Time

The man who referred to himself as Edward Smith moved carefully, not wanting to look like he was trying to avoid being seen, but also trying to make sure no one saw him. He was paranoid about being recognised. Facial prosthetics – fake eyebrows and different teeth - changed his appearance, as did the fresh scar on his face which tugged at his left eye to distort that side of his face slightly. However, he wasn't convinced it was enough to fool anyone who did more than glance in his direction. Members of the crew would recognise him. And he couldn't allow that.

Getting on board had been easier than expected. All it took was opportunity and a little patience, then a degree of luck to get past security by acting as a member of crew. Once inside the ship, he had the problematic paradox of needing to stay hidden while also needing to move around. Fortunately, his intimate knowledge of the ship and crew meant he could leverage several individuals, one of which he used to get on board, and another because there might be a need to throw people off his scent. Both believed his promises of rich rewards.

They were just lackeys though, brainless henchmen to go places he couldn't go and do the things he couldn't do. They were his eyes and ears above deck, reporting back to him while he worked below decks on things they couldn't know about and wouldn't understand.

This was his second excursion above the crew area at the bottom of the ship. Just like the last time, he was fearfully holding his breath and waiting to be spotted. This excursion was necessary, whereas the last one had been simply because he needed to see his work unfold, craved the satisfaction it gave him to see the disarray, confusion, and even horror he was able to cause. The people on board the ship had brought it on themselves and he felt not one jot of remorse for those he injured or terrorised.

It was going to get so much worse yet. What had gone before was just the very tip of the iceberg. He chuckled at his own choice of phrase.

His silent musings came to a sudden end when a noise interrupted them. Someone was coming in. He ducked quickly to the side to make sure he was out of sight and cursed his luck. The water sports centre was closed, why was there someone coming in? Glancing carefully around the side of the decompression chamber they had on board just in case it was ever needed, he held his breath as if the sound of his lungs extracting oxygen from the air would give his presence away. He recognised who it was but had to dredge his memory for the name: Special Rating Edgar Thomas.

The man calling himself Edward Smith needed to come here, it was vital to check he had access to everything he would require, and he'd been putting the task off for weeks. How typical that when he finally forced himself to take the risk, a member of the water sports team would choose the same time to make a visit.

He waited to see if Edgar would leave and ran through his list of tasks still needing attention. It was getting shorter. In the last almost three weeks he'd successfully accessed most of the vital systems on this ship. He couldn't do that without leaving a few tell-tale signs so he'd also messed with some of the systems which were not vital to make his careful fiddling look like random acts of vandalism. Hot water was one of them. Thousands of passengers and crew demanded the ship be able to supply a vast amount of hot water for cooking, cleaning, bathing, and other purposes. Shutting it off had created havoc and costly repairs while also damaging the name of the cruise line. Guests on board would remember the bad elements of their stay more than the good ones and would talk about them with more passion. They would remember the wonderful places they went but when they booked again, it would be with another cruise line because Purple Star had a terrible safety record and their maintenance was shocking. That is what they would tell their friends and write in online reviews.

Of course, damaging the reputation of the ship and the cruise line were nothing more than a by-product of his desire for revenge on the man who betrayed him. Alistair Huntley, captain of the Aurelia, would die soon enough, but not until he had seen all that he held dear crumble around him.

The mental image of Alistair Huntley lying dead at his feet gave him cause to smile, but his grin was short lived, wiped away by a memory of the other person he needed to kill. The interfering busybody who had no right ... no skill to have orchestrated his downfall. How she came to ruin his months of planning, he still had no idea, yet he'd watched her story with interest as she became involved in surprising event after surprising event and then the shocking story from Zangrabar where she inadvertently saved the Maharaja.

He was going to enjoy killing Patricia Fisher. Her and her friends. The list of people he intended to kill was not a long one. However, it wasn't short either. Arranged into tiers of importance, he wanted to work his way up to the top, but that wouldn't be possible. Patricia Fisher was in England and the ship was not. It would get to England, and he would disembark to find and kill her. In the meantime, he had much work to do on the Aurelia, carefully tapping into her delicate electronic systems.

'Hey, what are you doing down here?' The voice caught him by surprise. He'd been daydreaming about revenge instead of focussing on staying out of sight and hadn't noticed Edgar moving across the room.

He froze with his back to Edgar, unwilling to turn around as he cursed himself. He was wearing a crew uniform, but the generic deck one because it was the most common and therefore ignored in general. Wearing it, he could move about unnoticed among the other crew provided he kept his face hidden.

'Hey!' Edgar repeated, a little more forcefully now. 'I asked what you are doing down here. There's no reason for you to be in this area, I'm calling security.'

He couldn't allow that. Turning around, he held up the clip board he'd brought along as a prop, making sure it covered most of his face. 'There's no need for that,' he argued, trying to sound congenial. 'I was sent down here to get the things on this list,' he said, drawing Edgar's eyes to the clip board. Stuck to it was a form torn from a brochure. The man calling himself Edward Smith hoped it would fool people from a distance; no one was ever supposed to look at it.

Edgar glanced at it, and he frowned when what he saw wasn't a list at all. He flicked his eyes to the intruder's face and a question formed. 'Hey! I know you! You're …'

What Edgar was going to say died on his lips as the screwdriver he couldn't see behind the clipboard swept upwards. Seconds later, he tumbled to the deck, not quite dead, but very much dying.

Kneeling over his victim to check the job was done, he said, 'Yes, I am. But I don't use that name any longer. My new name,' he let an ironic smile tug the corner of his mouth, 'is Edward Smith.'

Grand Arrival

'Patty, what's going on?' Barbie's question captured the emotion of the moment perfectly.

I should have sensed there was something afoot when there were cars waiting for us at the airport. Purple Star Cruise Lines specialised in luxury, but they didn't throw their money away. Like any business, their shareholders expected to get a dividend at the end of the year and wouldn't tolerate frivolous expenditure. Which was why it surprised me to find three of the ship's limousines waiting for my party, the chauffeurs standing in a line as we came through the final set of security doors and into the arrivals lounge.

A large sign with my name on it proved impossible to miss, but the chauffeurs recognised me anyway. We were in Nova Scotia and tired after many, many hours of travelling.

Our flight to Montreal had been in the first-class area of the plane, the upgrade coming courtesy of the Maharaja of Zangrabar when he learned we were heading this way. Actually, he tried to buy me my own private airplane and, horrified at the idea, I talked him down to simply upgrading our tickets. It wasn't my first time flying first class, yet it also wasn't something I was used to and who doesn't love a little luxury? Poor Molly didn't know what to do with herself. My nineteen-year-old housemaid had only been on one holiday in her entire life; a girls week away in a budget resort on a shoestring budget. When they served her champagne, she asked for a plastic beaker because she was too terrified she might drop and break the expensive crystal glass it came in.

Now, after an hour in the car to get us from the airport to the seaport, the giant cruise ship loomed large in front of us, but all was not as we expected. I figured we would see a crowd of passengers filing aboard through the main entrance. We would be able to avoid the queue and board through the royal suites entrance located closer to the bow of the ship. However, while the crowd of passengers was exactly as expected, there was something odd going on at the smaller entrance my limousine was heading for.

A long, wide funnel of crew members in uniform were lined up on either side of the ornate awning that led through the sea door and into the ship. There had to be at least two hundred of them, consisting of security officers, stewards, maintenance, cleaning staff, chefs, and at the head of them all was the captain of the ship, Alistair Huntley. He was flanked by some of his senior officers, including his deputy captain, Commander Yusef. If that wasn't bad enough, a large band of the ship's musicians were assembled, and as the cars pulled to a stop, they launched into a fanfare to welcome our arrival.

Our arrival?

Who was I kidding? This was all for me, it had been organised by Alistair, and it was far too much. Security officers in their pristine white uniforms stepped forward to get the doors.

'It's Deepa,' squeaked Barbie, excited to see her friend again.

I spotted other faces I knew – Lieutenants Schneider and Baker were there, coming forward to greet us but acting as if I were a queen coming aboard in their stiff ceremonial movements.

The cold Canadian air bit at my skin when the doors swung open, and though I'd told myself to be ready for it, this close to the water, it was a good deal colder than I had anticipated.

'This is so much fun,' squeaked Barbie, sliding across the sumptuous leather to get out.

Poor Molly just looked bewildered. They sent three cars, but we all crammed into one because it seated six. It would have been impossible to divide us up otherwise. Both Wayne, my personal bodyguard appointed to watch over me by an anti-organised-crime squad in Scotland Yard, and Jermaine, my butler and all around ninja, insisted they had to remain at my side so they could be ready to defend me. I could never side-line Barbie and that just left Molly, the teenager on the trip of a lifetime with eyes like Alice down the rabbit hole.

Jermaine got out first, the band trumpeting even louder as his feet hit the tarmac.

'Are you sure you're not royalty, Mrs Fisher,' asked Molly, glued to her seat and terrified to get out where hundreds of people would see her.

Patting her knee, I tried to reassure her. 'Six months ago, I was cleaning other people's houses, Molly. I'm no more royal than anyone in this car. Just smile and try not to let the crowd worry you. We will be inside soon where we can relax.'

A yawn split her face. 'Good. I need a rest, Mrs Fisher. It feels like we've been travelling forever.' She wasn't wrong and the time difference wasn't helping. It was late afternoon here, but sometime just after breakfast where my brain was.

Wayne, Barbie, and Jermaine were all outside and it was my turn to exit the car. 'I'll go first,' I told my young charge. 'All the focus will be on me then.' With another pat to her knee, I let my two dogs, Anna and Georgie, plop out of the car and onto the tarmac where a cold breeze blew their fur instantly. They were going to need coats. They had been straining to get out since the car stopped, but now they were outside, and could feel the chill, they changed their minds.

Unfortunately, I was trying to get out as Anna decided the car was the place for her. Georgie followed her mum, the two dachshunds going either side of my leading foot as I tried to get it to the ground. All my weight was pitching forward as they pulled my foot back inside with their leads.

I grabbed for the top of the door and snagged it, but already out of control, I flailed helplessly, holding onto the door with one hand which made me spin around so I fell out of the car backwards. My feet came free simply due to inertia, yanking both dogs with me and their leads became tangled around my legs and right arm.

I said something colourful as I hit the ground, blushing because everyone watched me lose control and fall, including the band who likewise gasped and stopped playing. With no noise except my squeal and expletive, they all got to see and hear what a lady I am.

Now lying on my back with my feet still inside the car, and two dachshunds staring down at me with their tails wagging, I prayed the ground would open up and swallow me whole.

Molly's head appeared in my field of vision. 'Cor! That was spectacular, Mrs Fisher,' she let me know. 'Are you all right?'

Feet were rushing to help me right myself. Jermaine, Barbie, and Wayne had all moved away from the car to make way for the main attraction, and now they were coming back. My feet were stuck inside the car still which meant I either needed to do a backwards roll away from it which would give everyone a great shot of my bum. Or I needed to perform an insanely difficult ab crunch exercise to get back into the car.

Mercifully, I didn't have to do either because Jermaine scooped his arms under my shoulders and thighs, lifted me from the cold tarmac, and placed me gently back on my feet.

He put me down with my back to the crowd of onlookers, which helped a little given how crimson my face must look, but as the band started up again, I heard Alistair arriving.

'Patricia, my darling, are you all right? Did you hurt yourself?'

I bit my lip and forced calmness to flow through my body. With my friends either side of me, I turned to face my former lover and found myself startled by the care and compassion in his eyes. It almost made my knees weak, the same way it had when he first came to my aid. On that occasion, we hadn't yet met, and he was just being gentlemanly.

'I'm fine, Alistair. Thank you for coming out to greet us all. I think I would like to get inside now, if I may.'

Stewards arrived to collect our bags and cases, of which there were plenty, and Alistair offered me his arm to escort me down the funnel of crew to the ship's royal suites entrance. It all felt incredibly familiar.

Settling In

The ship was due to sail in just less than an hour, the sun beginning to set outside as the crew went through all their departure checks. In the Windsor Suite, a palatial accommodation intended to host royalty, I unclipped the dogs' leads and let them scamper. Anna acted as though we had come home, scampering away to explore the kitchen, and then whizzing across the carpet to visit one bedroom and then the next. Little Georgie, still small enough that she could easily run beneath her mother and barely the size of a guinea pig, raced after Anna with her legs blazing.

I put my handbag down on the elegant sideboard where I always used to put it when I was last here. Then, pausing, I looked around at the familiar space. Barbie came to stand beside me and slipped her hand into mine.

'How are you feeling, Patty? Is it weird to be back?' she asked.

I had to think about how I felt before I could answer her question. 'Yes and no, I guess,' I told her, finally. 'It feels as though I never left. It's only been a handful of weeks since I was last here in this room. I … I never thought I would come back. I think that is what is throwing me,' I admitted, managing to just about articulate the swirling emotions I felt. When the threat of the Godmother loomed and I had to find us somewhere to hide, the Aurelia presented itself as an instant and obvious answer. Not only was it constantly on the move and well away from anyone I knew who could conceivably get caught in a crossfire, there was an armed detachment of security guards on board and I knew they would defend me if it came to it.

'I'm glad we are back,' Barbie told me. 'It won't be for long and I get to see my friends again. Did you notice the ring on Deepa's finger?' she gushed.

Her question snapped my head and eyes around. 'She's engaged?' I asked, surprised by the news because I thought she was single.

Barbie beamed a big smile. 'She's going to come by later so we can get all the juicy gossip we've missed, but Martin proposed just a couple of days ago,' she revealed, naming Lieutenant Martin Baker. 'She knew we were coming so kept it a surprise.'

'That was quick. How long have they been seeing each other?'

'Just a couple of months. I think they got together in Zangrabar and … well it's a bit quick to be getting engaged, but they say that when you know, you know.' It was a cliché that had led to many couples getting married during the heady throes of early infatuation only to divorce painfully later, but they weren't children and maybe they had found 'the one'. I certainly hoped so and looked forward to congratulating her later.

'Can I bring you some refreshment, madam?' asked Jermaine. On arrival in our suite, he'd disappeared through the door in the kitchen to the attached butler's accommodation. His bags followed him, courtesy of three stewards, and now he was dressed in his full butler's livery, the official uniform issued by the Aurelia.

A smile curled the corners of my mouth. Now it felt like home. 'I think a gin and tonic might be in order, Jermaine.'

Molly came back out of her bedroom wearing a thong bikini that was little more than spaghetti straps with tiny triangles of material that only just covered her nipples. She had flip flops on her feet, a towel over her shoulder and a see-though bag containing a trashy magazine, sunglasses, her purse, and a dozen other items of paraphernalia she deemed necessary.

'Where's the nearest pool?' she asked.

Barbie's eyes flared and she mouthed, 'Wow,' in a direction only I would see, her comment referring to Molly's not-really-there swimsuit.

'You'll want an indoor pool for this leg,' I advised her. 'In fact, for this leg and the next couple. The outdoor pools are shut off for now. There's an indoor one on the next deck down.'

Barbie detached herself from my side, holding out her hand as she advanced on Molly. 'I'll show you where to go and how to find your way back. It's a big ship and we wouldn't want you getting lost on your first day.'

As they went to the door, Jermaine skipped ahead of them to open and close it, but found Agent Wayne Garrett outside just about to come in. He'd had to go through some paperwork with Commander Yusef regarding his status as the only armed person on board who was not a member of the ship's security. It had been arranged in advance, so the paperwork was nothing more than a formality. Task complete, he was back with me and wanted to inspect the suite.

'Please, go ahead,' I welcomed him. 'That's your bedroom over there.' He followed my arm to a door and went inside, reappearing a few moments later when a knock on the suite's door caught his attention.

Wayne stalked toward the lobby area with a hand on the holster of his gun. Hidden inside his jacket, I was glad he didn't see fit to brandish it in readiness when Jermaine answered the door. More stewards filed in carrying yet more luggage.

Wayne relaxed, or rather, he took his hand off his gun. I touched his arm to get his attention which made him flinch as if jabbed with an electric probe. In turn, his response made me jump, my hand going to my heart as I too flinched.

'Goodness, Wayne. You have got to relax. We are safe here. The Godmother has no idea where we have gone and no way of finding out. It will give us time to regroup while the police track her organisation down. No one is coming to the door to kill me, and if they do, I doubt they will knock first.'

He eyed me sceptically. 'Safe here, huh, Mrs Fisher? I heard a few stories about events in this suite.' My face blushed, remembering Alistair's late-night visits and wondering what events he might have heard about. 'Didn't one of the walls get peppered with bullets?'

I laughed as relief washed over me; he was referring to a different kind of event altogether. 'Yes,' I admitted. 'This one.' I pointed to my bedroom. 'A rather unpleasant chap called Maurice tried to shoot the people in my suite by shooting through the wall of my bedroom. Looking about, I then pointed to another wall. 'That one got shot too.' I took a couple of paces. 'Then over at this desk, Jermaine almost got his head bashed in. Next to that couch,' I pointed to one of a pair, 'that is where a terrorist from East Houptiou tried to kill me.' Now reeling off a list of deadly encounters, I stopped myself and accepted that Wayne might have a point. 'Okay, well, we should be safe from the Godmother.'

He pursed his lips. 'But isn't this where you first encountered her?' he pointed out.

'Not quite. I've never met her.' I thought about my statement. 'I've never knowingly met her,' I corrected myself. 'I accidentally got in the way of her illegal business dealings when I stopped gangsters killing each other and everyone else after we left Miami, and then again when the ship docked in Tokyo. That was all their fault too. They made me stop them. I wanted to go sightseeing with my friends. I even tried to go to Mount Fuji, but they kidnapped me and forced me to do their bidding under threat of killing Jermaine and my ex-husband. My only way out was to wreck their entire organisation.'

'The Godmother isn't taking that into consideration,' Wayne reminded me.

Jermaine handed me a cold glass of crisp, delicious Hendricks gin paired with slimline tonic, ice, and cucumber. It was sublime.

Another knock at the door interrupted our discussion and I was thankful for it; no good could come from scrutinising the past. I needed to focus on the future and how I was going to beat the Godmother at her own game.

Jermaine's voice echoed through from the lobby. 'Captain Huntley. I shall announce you.' My butler came back into the room, and though it was completely unnecessary, I knew he lived for the pomp and ceremony of his role, so I waited patiently for him to announce my visitor. 'Captain Alistair Huntley, madam.'

'Thank you, Jermaine,' I replied with a small dip of my head. Then to Alistair, 'Won't you please join me?' I moved to a couch and sat, upright and with my knees together as a lady ought, placing my beverage on a crystal coaster while Alistair handed Jermaine his hat.

He came to join me, taking a seat opposite as if sensing that I was not as warm to him as he were to me. 'Hello, Patricia,' he said as he relaxed onto his couch. 'I only have a few minutes.'

I raised a hand to stop him. 'It's perfectly all right, Alistair. 'The ship is about to sail, and you must get to the bridge. I understand completely. How have you been?' I was being conversational.

'Lonely,' he admitted, surprising me. 'I missed you, Patricia, and I don't mind admitting it.'

I had a bone to pick with him and felt that if I didn't address the issue now, it would soon be too late. 'The ceremony outside was too much, Alistair,' I told him bluntly. 'It was embarrassing for me.' I watched his face colour. 'Please, do not do that again. I can make a spectacle of myself without anyone's help.'

He bowed his head and lowered his eyes to the deck. 'I'm sorry, Patricia. I had hoped it would act as a demonstration of my affection for you.'

'It was too much,' I repeated. Then I softened, feeling like I was beating the man up for no good reason. 'Just promise you won't go overboard for me again, please.'

'Of course,' he replied. It didn't take him long to gather himself. He hadn't intended to disappoint or upset me, his shame for doing so passing swiftly. 'Will you join me for dinner tonight?' he asked.

I expected the question and had my answer prepared. Coming back on board I was both thrilled and concerned that he might wish to resume our relationship as if no time had passed. I could admit to myself a desire to fall straight back into the handsome man's arms, but I also felt caution was necessary if I didn't intend to stay there. I was on board to evade the Godmother's attempts to kill me and find time to think my way out of her clutches, not to rekindle our relationship. If I were to go to him tonight, what would happen when the danger from the Godmother was passed? I would go home and break both his and my heart yet again. Maybe it would be worse this time. I didn't know, but I was here and back in this suite because he made it happen. It took one phone call to arrange so how could I refuse to meet him for dinner?

I said, 'I would love to, Alistair. I will be joined by my personal bodyguard, Agent Garrett of Scotland Yard.'

A frown creased Alistair's forehead momentarily. It was gone no sooner than it appeared, but it showed me the disappointment he felt because a gooseberry to join us was not his expectation.

Before he could answer, his radio crackled and a message I never expected to hear again reached my ears and his at the same time.

'Secretary, secretary, secretary. Deck three, storeroom twenty-six, out.'

Problems Onboard

The coded message was intended to reach all members of crew tuned to the security channel and be such that they would know what it meant, but no passengers within earshot would understand its significance.

Alistair was on his feet in a heartbeat, but I wasn't far behind him. He had his radio in his hand as he ran for the door. 'This is the captain. I am on route. Out.'

Wayne appeared from his bedroom. 'Are you going out, Mrs Fisher?' he asked flippantly, since he could see me running after the captain. 'I have asked that you let me know when you plan to leave the suite.'

'I'm leaving the suite!' I called loudly over my shoulder.

Alistair had the door open and was out in the corridor already. 'Patricia, you ought not to come with me.'

'That's what you always said before,' I reminded him as we both turned right and ran for the elevators. 'Tell me, Alistair. Have there been any murders or deaths since I left the ship?'

A couple coming toward us had to duck to one side to allow us passage. Alistair calling his thanks to them instead of answering my question, but at the elevator, where we had no option but to pause, he pulled a face and said, 'No.'

'None?'

'Not one,' he replied, almost apologising for the death rate dropping markedly since I left. 'We have had a couple of heart attacks and a stroke though,' he added as if that made a difference. The elevator arrived, a gaggle of passengers alighting, most likely heading for the upper deck restaurant where I planned to eat later. It was a little early for dinner in my opinion and my body clock was a mess with jetlag.

Wayne, my mostly silent companion, asked which floor button to push with his hand held next to the control panel.

'Deck,' I corrected him.

'I'm sorry,' he replied, not understanding me.

I leaned forward to jab number two and explained, 'It's a ship. One gets floors in a building. This is a ship and they are decks.' The light didn't come on when I pressed it, and I remembered that passengers couldn't access the lower six decks of the ship. A code was needed. Wordlessly, Alistair stepped up to the panel, punched in his access number and pressed the number two once more. This time, the elevator started to move.

'You know,' said Alistair, 'having had time to think, we haven't had any deaths, but there has been a spate of 'accidents' that were not accidents at all.' I gave him a look that told him he needed to expand on his statement because he was just being cryptic. He grimaced as he answered. 'I think I have a saboteur on board.'

I didn't have a chance to ask him anything else about what specifically that meant because the elevator arrived on deck two.

'How far are we from storeroom twenty-six?' I asked, knowing the ship was over a thousand feet long and it could be quite a hike to get from one point to another depending on where they were relative to each other.

'It's not too far,' he replied, failing to give any real indication of distance. 'Storeroom twenty-six is just bow side of midships.' Since we were at the bow end, we probably had less than five hundred feet to go. It took about five minutes through the twisting, winding passageways.

I could hear the crew gathered outside the storeroom before we got there, turning another corner brought them into view. It was mostly white uniforms, the ship's security responding to the report of a body, but there were two men dressed in the dark blue of the maintenance team also present.

Seeing his captain approaching, Lieutenant Baker snapped out a crisp salute and began to report as Alistair returned it.

'Sir, the deceased is Engineer First class Edgar Thomas. We haven't moved him yet, sir, and he's only been touched to confirm he is dead.' Having delivered his report, Baker flicked his eyes to me and dipped his head with a fleeting smile.

'The nature of his death?' Alistair asked, all business and no emotion.

Baker's reply came without hesitation. 'Murder, sir. The weapon is still embedded in his skull. I think we can rule out accidental impalement.'

'Oh? Why is that?' the captain asked.

Again, Baker had an easy answer lined up. 'He's been moved, sir. There isn't enough blood here for this to be where the attack took place. His wound has bled plenty but other than what is on his clothing, there isn't much blood to be seen.'

Alistair pursed his lips. 'Show me.'

Lieutenant Baker led him inside and I followed, never questioning whether I ought to as I approached the body. Wayne caught my arm. 'Mrs Fisher, there is no reason for you to involve yourself in ship's business. It would be safer for you in your suite.'

I tugged my arm free and shot him a warning look. 'Agent Garrett I shall thank you for not touching me unless you are actively saving my life. As for my safety: I am safer here below decks surrounded by the ship's security, than I am anywhere on board this ship. Staying in one place, such as my suite, for too long, provides anyone who wishes me harm a position to target, so you can rest assured I will be on the move the whole time we are on board and may sleep elsewhere than my own bed for the same reason.'

Feeling Agent Garrett had been suitably told, I turned away and caught up with Alistair, who I then realised, from the small smile on his face, had overheard my comment about sleeping elsewhere and assumed he was meant to hear it.

To avoid meeting his eyes, I pushed around him to see poor Mr Thomas. He wore canvas trousers and a polo shirt showing the Aurelia's water sports centre logo. The left side of the shirt was soaked with blood, enough of it that I had to instantly agree with Baker's assessment of the body being moved since there was almost none on the deck. 'Did he have family?' I asked,

'No, Mrs Fisher,' said Lieutenant Pippin, stepping forward. I hadn't seen him among the guards outside the ship when we arrived and hadn't realised until now.

I squealed, 'Pippin!' gleefully and pulled the young man into a hug. To me, though I would never say it, he looked too young to be on the security team. There was nothing worth shaving on his chin, but he wasn't much younger than Barbie. Having suitably embarrassed the young man, I let him go and went back to looking at the body.

Pippin continued, 'He is divorced, according to our records, though his ex-wife is still listed as his next of kin.'

Alistair sniffed. 'That probably means he has no family. He's a Welshman, yes?'

Pippin nodded. 'Yessir.'

Alistair nodded his head as he thought and blew out a frustrated breath. 'Anything else?' he asked. 'Have you a team searching for the site of the murder?'

'Not yet, sir. I planned to have the entire second deck searched shortly. It seems probable he was moved only a short distance - he is not a light man.'

Alistair made no comment, instead asking, 'Any sign of our saboteur?'

Lieutenant Baker raised an eyebrow. 'You believe Thomas might have disturbed him, sir?'

Alistair continued to stare at his dead crewmember. 'It is just one possibility. We must consider why he was killed. It was a violent murder, but not an emotional one. There is a single wound which suggests the killer was doing what they believed to be necessary.'

I nodded my head, impressed with his interpretation. My thoughts were the same, though I hadn't connected the saboteur yet. Alistair didn't get around to explaining what that was about yet.

As if jolted into action, Alistair stepped away. 'Very good, Mr Baker. Please transfer Mr Thomas to the morgue and open an investigation separate to that of the ongoing saboteur case. I want them to be given your undivided attention, understood?'

'Yes, sir,' replied Lieutenant Baker. 'Are you not going to delay departure to repatriate the body, sir?'

Alistair had been turning away, but he paused to answer the question. 'Not this time, Mr Baker. I want the body here so we can investigate. If this is the work of our saboteur, I want to make sure we have the evidence to hand when we catch him.' The Aurelia operated like a nation of its own. Separated from law enforcement agencies and not associated with any of them anyway, they fell under Bahamian law because the ship was registered there. If they needed additional support, it would come from there, but pride prevented captains from calling for help, so the crew, the security detachment especially, fended for themselves when crimes occurred.

Baker said, 'Very good, sir,' and shifted his focus to deal with poor Mr Thomas.

Leaving the storeroom with Wayne in my shadow, I asked Alistair about the saboteur. 'What has he or she damaged so far? What makes you convinced it is deliberate?'

Alistair didn't break pace to answer my question, we were walking side by side, making our way back to the nearest elevator, but he began to gesticulate. 'It's mostly minor so far. Annoying things such as shutting off the hot water production for decks seven to ten and gluing the controls so the maintenance team had to manufacture new parts. Also, the fire alarm system command wire was severed in more than a dozen places, each of them obscure and hard to find. That was one of the worst because we were in port and had a twenty-four-hour delay in sailing because we cannot, by law, put to sea when the fire system isn't operable.'

'One of the worst,' I echoed. 'How many incidents have there been?'

'Twenty-three so far,' he replied, failing to hide the irritation he felt. 'Everything from dye getting into the passengers' laundry to ruin it, to shutting off the air-conditioning to the bridge when we were off the coast of Florida, and all the way up to the bilge pumps wedged open so the ship begins to flood.' He saw the shock on my face and smiled. 'Don't worry. It's not as dangerous as it sounds. Warning buzzers sound almost instantly. There were a few feet of water in a couple of sections. This old girl wouldn't begin to sink until more than ten sections were filled.'

'Do you think this person might be Edgar's killer?' I asked.

I got a smile in return. 'Isn't it your job to work that out?' he joked. 'I'm not sure what to think,' he admitted when his smile faded. 'It has to be a member of the crew.'

'What makes you so sure?' I wanted to know.

We reached a pair of elevators, where we had to wait for a car. It was one of the crew elevators which only travelled between decks seven and one - one being the lowest – so we wouldn't have long to wait. It gave Alistair a chance to answer though. 'The sabotage is all happening below the passenger level. That might be considered indication enough because of the number of security measures in place to stop passengers accidentally accessing the crew levels. However, the damage being done has targeted specific systems at specific times when they are either vulnerable, or likely to be unmanned or, like with the fire system command wire, cause the maximum amount of damage or stress. I think that not only is it a crew member, but it is also someone who knows the ship well.' He lowered his voice to speak secretively even though we were in the elevator. 'I have my security teams watching the engineering team; they are the ones most able to do the damage we have been suffering, they are the ones with the knowledge.' He raised his voice again as the car reached level seven. 'Of course, it could be anyone, which is why we are struggling to do anything about it.'

Turning to look down at my eyes once we were back in the passageway, Alistair said, 'I really must get to the bridge now. It would seem I have a busy few hours ahead of me. If you are able, I would like to eat dinner together later, but failing that, perhaps a nightcap?' he suggested hopefully.

Alistair was no fool. He recognised that he'd come on too strong and he was backing off. Backing off but not backing away. He knew what he wanted, and it was me. He once said I was a prize worth waiting for, and he was still waiting.

I felt like taking his hand to give him some comfort, but I kept my hands together, still unsure about how I felt. 'Let me know when your duties for the day are finished.' It was a non-committal thing to say and we both knew it, yet he accepted my answer with a slight nod of his head and left me in Wayne's silent care.

'Shall we return to your suite, Mrs Fisher?' Wayne asked, breaking his silence for the first time in more than half an hour. 'Or would you like to show me around? I have the impression you know this ship rather well.' He made the suggestion with a smile and in a way I couldn't resist.

To be back on board was a lot like I had never left. I was staying in the same suite with Jermaine as my butler once more. Barbie was with me again and so were the members of the crew I got to know during my previous visit. Any moment now, I expected Lady Mary Bostihill-Swank to totter around the corner half sloshed on gin. Thinking about my socialite friend, I almost took out my phone to message her, but stopped myself. My friends and I had all agreed a simple rule while we were on board: no communication with the outside world. None whatsoever. If no one knew where we were, then no one could let it slip.

A slight judder let me know the ship had set sail, its mighty engines churning the water to propel it onward from Nova Scotia to our next stop in Greenland. I needed a drink. 'Come along Agent Garrett,' I replied as I started walking. 'I'll start you off with a tour of the bars. First though, I need to make sure the final member of our team got on board. I haven't heard from him.'

Wayne gave me a confused look. 'What final member?'

Mystery Guest

I hadn't told anyone. Not even Jermaine or Barbie, who I kept almost no secrets from. In their case, I kept the secret because it would be a fun surprise, in the case of my appointed bodyguard, I elected to forget to tell him because I didn't want him attempting to argue. Not that I knew he would, only that I suspected he might.

I led him through the ship on deck seven until we reached roughly the middle of the ship and there, I turned a corner to bring us to a bank of elevators. 'Wow,' he said. 'You really do know your way around.'

'I got to learn a lot of it while people were chasing me,' I told him with a wry smile. 'One tends to quickly memorise the escape routes when survival depends upon it.'

'Do you plan to tell me who the mystery guest is, Mrs Fisher?' Agent Garrett's tone held a tinge of frustration. He wanted to be in charge and order me around while claiming it was for my own safety. That wasn't going to happen, and it pleased me that he was intuitive enough to recognise pushing me wouldn't work. Nevertheless, my choice to keep him in the dark undermined his ability to keep me safe, or so he believed, and it was manifesting in borderline anger now.

I made a show of pursing my lips to one side as if I were considering his request but shook my head. 'No. I don't think I shall. The name wouldn't mean much to you anyway; you have never met him.'

More guests joined us just before the elevator arrived on our deck so there were six of us travelling upward.

'Which deck?' asked Wayne of the four passengers, getting his terminology right.

'All the way to the top, young man,' said a bubbly Canadian lady in her late sixties. 'We have reservations in the top deck restaurant, and I am gonna eat me some lobster!' she guffawed heartily. She had an effervescent character and the cork was well and truly out of the bottle.

'The sushi is especially good,' I remarked conversationally.

'Oh, have you been on board long, honey?' she asked, 'And where are your delightful accents from. Are you British?'

'English,' I corrected her. 'And we arrived this afternoon, but this isn't my first time on board.'

'Well, lucky you. We had to save to come on this trip, but I'm going royal watching after dinner.'

Unable to help myself, I bit her bait. 'Royal watching?'

She leaned over to whisper as if it were a secret. 'I think the Queen of England came on board earlier. 'I couldn't see all that well from our little window, but there was a big parade at a private entrance at the front of the ship and an old lady got out of a procession of cars and she had little dogs with her. She was met by the captain himself. I saw it!' she insisted, but her final remark wasn't aimed at me, it was to her husband and the other couple who hadn't seen it and didn't believe her.

I elected to keep quiet.

We got off on the nineteenth deck, wishing our elevator companions an enjoyable evening as we went in separate directions. Though I could tell Wayne was itching to press me to tell him who the mystery guest was, I wasn't sure he was even on board. With the events in London just yesterday – I couldn't believe it was only yesterday – and then all the travel, when I knew he was also travelling, neither of us had messaged the other for an update. However, I felt sure I would have heard something if he were not here.

Checking the number on the door, I knocked twice and waited.

We both heard a voice on the other side. It was a man's voice and sounded like he was shouting to someone else in the cabin. Wayne cut his eyes in my direction for suddenly we were talking about more than one mystery guest. Or so he thought.

The door was flung open by the exuberant person on the other side and a beaming smile cut straight to my heart. 'Mrs Fisher! We're on a big boat, and we went on a plane! This is so much fun!'

I couldn't help the laugh that burst from my lips as I said, 'Hi, Sam.'

He backed away from the door, inviting me inside with a swish of his arm and calling to his parents, 'Mum! Dad! Mrs Fisher is here!'

I turned my head toward the bedroom, expecting they would be in there unpacking as they were not in sight, but a flicker of movement revealed that they were on the balcony. The door opened with a blast of frigid air as they hurried back into the warmth of their suite. Melissa and Paul Chalk were friends from the village. I'd gone to school with Paul's younger sister, that was how the connection came about but the bond was with Melissa who was pregnant with Sam on one of my more painful failed pregnancies. She went on to have Sam and I lost mine shortly after we discovered we were both due around the same time. Sam was born with Downs Syndrome which meant that at thirty he still lived with his parents. It also meant that certain elements of his mental and cognitive abilities did not function quite like other people. I thought he was brilliant. He was funny, permanently positive, full of spirit, and reliable. When I needed an assistant in my detective business, I hadn't hesitated to hire him.

Melissa had shoulder length brown hair with a natural wave she generally moaned about because it made it hard to tame into any style she was happy with. At five feet seven inches tall, she was average height. She had brown eyes, small boobs, and hips that were a touch wider than she liked. Her husband, Paul, had been with her since they were teenagers and seemed just as in love now as he was back then. His sandy coloured hair was receding fast like a tide going out on a shallow beach. He was tall and thin and sported a pot belly where too many Sunday afternoon football matches in front of the television had been enjoyed with a few beers. They were a life-sized demonstration of how little a person needs in order to be happy.

My assistant, Sam, had an unruly mop of brown hair and facial features that showed his Downs, but all that was lost behind a perpetual smile which even now creased his face as we came inside the Chalks' suite and closed the door.

'How was your journey?' I asked of the lengthy process of getting to Canada. Normal people would wait for a cruise ship to arrive in their own country. Running away from the Godmother hadn't given me that option and Sam had to come along because she might target him for his connection to me.

Melissa hurried across the suite to get to me, almost running so she could sweep me into a hug. 'Oh, Patricia, this is so wonderful,' she gushed. 'We haven't had a proper holiday for years. Well, you know I was never really able to work with Sam at the house most of the time, so there was never enough money left over, but this … this is something else. We would never have been able to afford this if we saved until the day we died. I don't know how we could ever repay you,' she said as she stepped back again.

Alone in my own personal space once more, I chuckled for I knew how I felt the first morning when I awoke on the ship and found myself constantly marvelling at how incredible it all was. They were in a smaller suite than me, but then so was everyone on the ship. However, the family suites on the nineteenth deck were plush and wide and came with a balcony which they had just explored. When she hugged me, her clothing had still been freezing cold.

'I'm glad you are here,' I replied to her excited outburst. 'All I did was ask a favour of a friend. I'm sorry you have to be here because of me.' I'd explained why they needed to come away and was thankful they hadn't argued. To them, the Godmother was an invisible threat they'd only heard of because their son and I were nearly run off the road by her assassins and because Angelica Howard-Box's house got shot into swiss cheese. Nevertheless, they were here, and with luck, they would enjoy a few weeks' vacation at no cost.

'Be here because of you?' Melissa repeated. 'Stuck in these depressing palatial surroundings with incredible food and incredible sights and more luxury than I know what to do with. I'm booked in for a spa treatment in an hour,' she boasted.

Remembering Wayne was standing behind me at the door, I introduced him. 'This is Agent Wayne Garrett. He's my copper, you might say.' Wayne waved hello to the Chalks. 'He's on loan from Scotland Yard to keep me safe. If it's alright with you, I thought I might borrow Sam for a while. We have a mystery to solve,' I added at the last moment, then wished I hadn't. I knew it would excite Sam to think we were detectives again, but I had no intention of investigating the recently discovered murder.

Sam needed no further encouragement, of course. He ran to his bedroom, returning a few seconds later wearing a jacket and tie.

Melissa shot me a look that said it was too late for me to change my mind now. 'I guess Sam is going with you. Have fun, Sam.' She turned to inspect her son, brushed some lint from his jacket and had a go at straightening his hair, giving up with a resigned smile a moment later when it refused to be tamed. Wayne opened the door when I indicated it was time to go, and we set off once more, Sam bouncing out into the passageway in his usual excited manner.

As he dashed forward to the elevators when I told him we were heading up one deck, Wayne quietly remarked, 'Any more surprise mystery guests, Mrs Fisher?'

I shot him a grin which I hoped was answer enough because I had no intention of telling him, or anyone else, about the person staying on deck eight.

Royalty

I led Sam and Wayne to the upper deck restaurant where a large bar next to the panoramic front windows provided an incredible view of the Canadian coastline going by. I was recognised by a steward on the way in and offered a table of my choice when I was ready for dinner. I sent Jermaine and Barbie a message to let them know where I was and hoped Molly hadn't gotten herself lost already as Barbie predicted. I expected Barbie would be catching up with old friends.

At the bar, I ordered water for Wayne, a gin and tonic for myself and a virgin pina colada for Sam. His drink came with an umbrella which blew his mind away. Taking a sip of my drink, I caught sight of a woman who looked away the instant I spotted her. She'd been staring at me from across the bar, standing next to a man I assumed was her husband.

I turned away, dismissing the notion that she was watching me as silly. She probably just thought I looked like someone she knew.

Having waited patiently, Sam asked, 'What is the mystery, Mrs Fisher?'

It was my own fault. In my happiness to see him, I'd blurted it out and now I had to do something about it. It occurred to me that I could lie and say I'd just said that so his parents would let him come with me, but that felt wrong. And I couldn't for the life of me make something up on the spot that we could investigate and solve, so I lowered my voice, and told him, 'There might be a killer on board, Sam.'

His eyes widened as he sipped his drink. Spitting out his straw, he asked, 'Are we going to catch him, Mrs Fisher?'

'Well,' I took a gulp of cold gin and set my glass back on the bar. In doing so, I saw the woman look away again and narrowed my eyes. I wasn't imagining it, but should I be paranoid about someone watching me? She looked like a passenger on holiday with her husband. Maybe she knew who I was from television and newspaper stories. Forcing myself to dismiss it, I went back to Sam. 'The Aurelia has its own security force. They are responsible for sorting out any crimes that happen on board.'

'Like the police?' Sam tried to clarify.

'Yes, Sam. A lot like the police. They will have to work out what happened to the man who was killed and try to find out who did it.'

'Isn't that your job?' he asked, looking confused at the concept that someone else might solve a crime. He used the exact same phrase Alistair joked with earlier.

'Not this time, Sam,' I replied. Then seeing his disappointed look, I added, 'But maybe you and I should look into things a bit to see if we can help them to solve it.'

He drained his glass with one last almighty suck and placed it back on the bar with a determined thump. 'I'm ready, Mrs Fisher,' he claimed, whipping a magnifying glass from an inside jacket pocket, together with a notebook and pen for making notes, just like I'd taught him.

'Oh, my goodness, Sam!' squealed Barbie, bouncing into view and sweeping my young charge into a hug. Barbie tended to forget the effect she had on men, crushing her ample chest against Sam, and holding him. Sam might have Downs, but he was still a man and she was still a ridiculously attractive woman. Letting him go, she turned to me with an accusing look. 'Patty, you never said Sam was coming.'

I took a moment to turn Sam toward the bar. 'Sam why don't you catch the barman's eye and get us a fresh round of drinks. I'm sure Barbie would like something.' That would keep him busy and facing forward while the lump in his trousers dissipated. 'Sorry, Barbie. I thought it was fun to keep a surprise up my sleeve.'

She grinned at me. 'You are so sneaky, Patty.' Remembering something, her smile vanished, and she leaned in closer. 'Did you hear the coded message earlier?'

I blew a breath out through my nose and wondered if I should tell her. 'Did you know a chap in the water sports centre called Edgar Thomas?'

She skewed her lips to one side. 'How do you know who it was already, Patty? You're supposed to be taking it easy here and staying out of trouble while the police catch the Godmother. And no, that's not someone I know. Is that who it was?'

I nodded, pausing our conversation for a moment to assist Sam in placing the drinks order. 'What would you like?' I asked Barbie.

She spied my balloon glass of melting ice and cucumber. 'Same as you, I think.'

The drinks came and I passed one to her, using the moment to check across the bar where the woman was no longer visible. It had been my paranoia. Dismissing it, I turned back to Barbie and found the woman, and her husband, standing just behind her.

We locked eyes and the woman's cheeks coloured instantly. 'Oh, gosh,' she stammered in an embarrassed way. 'I'm so sorry. I'm interrupting rudely.' She seemed flustered and was now trying to reverse direction to get away. She bumped into her husband, a tall man with a hooked beak nose and a hair line that had receded so far it was touching the collar of his jacket. He looked bewildered by his wife's behaviour and I got the impression he'd spent decades of marriage trailing along behind in her wake because it was the only way to achieve a peaceful life.

The woman was English, from Bristol perhaps, and my age, or thereabouts: somewhere in her early fifties certainly. I could have let her push her husband out of the way and watch her retreat to safety, but something had convinced her to come to see me and now I wanted to know what it was.

'Hello,' I called, raising my voice slightly and making it sound inviting. 'I'm Patricia.'

The woman had managed to get her back to me in her haste to escape and would have gotten away if her husband hadn't acted as a barrier. She froze and turned around to face me. 'I'm so sorry, Your Highness.'

'I told you not to come over here,' the man moaned.

I held up an index finger. 'I'm sorry. I have no idea what is going on. You addressed me as Your Highness.'

The woman's cheeks were blushing scarlet now. Her hair was perfectly straight in a dark auburn tone that looked natural and matched her eyebrows. It was cut to hang six inches below her shoulders. She had green eyes hidden behind thick-rimmed glasses that came with a chain around her neck to keep them in place. She was short, perhaps five feet one or two which made her starkly short against her husband who had to be close to six and a half feet tall, and she was a little rounded at the hips where he was straight up and down.

Looking like she wanted to be anywhere else but standing in front of me, her expression changed from embarrassment to confusion as she processed my comment. Speaking quietly, she said, 'I saw you arrive,' she revealed knowingly. 'The big procession and the band and everything. Are you here incognito?'

I had to wonder how many other people had seen the grand arrival and watched to see if there was a mega popstar or a famous politician arriving. Fixing a smile, I accepted that the woman had only been staring at me earlier because she was trying to work out who I was. It didn't explain why she approached me but maybe she'd hoped to get a photograph with someone famous. I'd met plenty of people on board who spent their time celebrity spotting.

'I'm just Patricia,' I told her. 'I know the captain,' I added, hoping that would explain the band and the hundreds of crew who turned out in the cold to greet me. 'We're, um … old friends,' I tried. 'He went a bit overboard, but really, there's nothing special about me.'

She looked surprised for a moment, but then gave me a knowing smile. 'Your secret is safe with me, Your Highness.' She didn't believe what I told her. She assumed it was my attempt at covering up the truth, and before I had a chance to say anything more, she gave her husband a shove to get him moving and was swallowed by a press of fresh passengers trying to get to the bar.

I looked at Barbie, shaking my head in amused disbelief. Matching my smile, she clinked her glass against mine and said, 'Bottoms up.' As I lifted my glass to my lips, she cheekily added, 'Your Highness.'

I almost snorted my drink as we shared a laugh, but a tortured sound at high decibels prevented any further chance of conversation. It was a klaxon sounding over the PA system and in the first second of its sounding, everyone in sight froze rigidly to the spot.

Then a loud, robotic voice said, 'Abandon ship! Abandon ship! All crew to the lifeboat stations!'

Abandon Ship!

The message switched back to the klaxon for two seconds before repeating itself and settling into a loop. Nobody moved for a heartbeat, worried faces looking at their loved ones in question, and then everyone seemed to move at once, an explosion of arms and legs as people scrambled for the restaurant exit.

I grabbed Sam's arm to pull him out of the way as people ran by. They would have knocked into him or maybe even run over him as their herd mentality took control.

Barbie shook her head and frowned deeply. 'That's not the emergency message,' she stated. 'No one would ever be stupid enough to tell everyone to abandon the ship. It would just create panic.' Which is what it was very effectively doing. The bar workers were making their way out from behind the bar to follow the press of people running for the exit.

Barbie climbed onto a barstool and raised her arms. She stood high above everyone else when she shouted, 'Everyone stop! There is no need to panic. This is a prank!'

A few people looked her way, but most couldn't even hear her above the din of passengers and crew trying to get out.

Sounding worried, Sam asked, 'What do we do, Mrs Fisher?'

I picked up my glass from the bar. 'We finish our drinks, Sam,' I replied stiffly. Through my feet I could feel the ship was still on an even keel. There had been no sound of a problem preceding the emergency announcement, but then I remembered the saboteur, and Alistair talking about the bilge pumps being switched off. From my limited knowledge, the pump ejected water that gathered in the bowels of the ship. When they failed to function, the ship very, very slowly filled with water. It was only if the ship had a leak that their failure might become a problem. However, with a saboteur on board, what else might he do? Could he jam a sea cock open? The bilge pumps pushed the water out through one-way valves, but a valve can be damaged, right? Was there frigid ocean filling the lower levels of the ship while I calmly sipped my gin and tonic. Ice in my drink is one thing, but I have no wish to bathe in it.

Moving closer to Barbie, I quickly told her about the series of 'accidents' the Aurelia had recently suffered. Her mouth formed a shocked O shape and her eyes flared as she considered what that could mean.

While we both fretted about the ramifications of the ship actually starting to sink, Sam tugged my sleeve. 'Mrs Fisher, I think I should try to find my parents. They might be worried.'

Of course. I hadn't thought this through at all. 'You're absolutely right, Sam. Let's get you back to them.'

Barbie climbed the bar, leaning over it so her pert bottom was uppermost before swinging back down with a ship's phone in her hand. 'What's their cabin number?' she asked.

I gave her it, and she nodded approvingly. 'Nineteenth deck. Nice.' With the phone at her ear, she waited patiently, but it didn't take long for her eyes to tell me what I expected to hear. 'The lines are jammed,' she told us.

It came as no surprise. 'Right,' I said, sounding determined as I took Sam's hand in mine. 'Let's make our way back to your suite, shall we, young man?'

Our drinks were left on the bar as we joined the throng still trying to get through the logjam at the restaurant doors. People were screaming and shouting and getting excited. A pair of ship's security were doing their best to corral people but their voices were lost in the hubbub of noise.

The tannoy bleeped twice, the first new noise since the emergency announcement started. Then a calm voice spoke over the sound of the wailing klaxon. 'This is your captain speaking. There is no emergency. The ship is not ailing and there is no need to go outside into the cold. What you are hearing has been caused by an electrical fault. It is being addressed now.' His voice was difficult to hear over the constant noise of the klaxon, so much so that I doubted anyone stuck in the press of people could hear it. 'Please all remain calm. This issue will be resolved momentarily.' Just like that the emergency call for everyone to abandon the ship stopped and an eerie silence settled over the room as everyone stopped fighting and yelling simultaneously. Even the two security guards stopped to see what might happen next.

Alistair's voice returned, this time clear and crisp and easy to understand. 'This is Captain Alistair Huntley.' He repeated his earlier message, making it clear the warning system suffered an electric fault. He apologised to everyone on board, crew and passengers alike, and opened all bars and restaurants for free drinks to be served for the next hour – a ploy to get anyone outside back into the warm.

There would be injuries, that I was certain of. I'd witnessed men throwing punches in their bid to escape the restaurant and this was just one small part of the ship. What had happened below decks? Had anyone foolishly jumped from the ship and tried to swim to the shore? The sun was down but lights were still visible in the distance. I prayed that would not be the case.

No one seemed to know what to do. The alarm had stopped and the voice that replaced it sounded genuine. Do we abandon ship or not? Some people had been in the middle of their meal when the madness started, a few drifted back and retook their seats. It encouraged more to do the same, but there were others who didn't trust the second announcement and wanted to get to the lifeboats now in case this was a ruse. Someone shouted that there weren't enough lifeboats, reminding people of the Titanic, and a fresh surge of panic broke out.

Fortunately, the captain's message was reinforced in person by fresh crew members arriving. They were led by Commander Yusef, the deputy captain. He begged for calm and managed to quieten the dissenting voices by assuring them that no one would stop them if they wished to wait outside. The temperature is just below freezing he reminded them before moving on in a dismissive way to join those looking pensive but, nevertheless, behaving themselves at the bar and tables of the restaurant.

'Do you believe the bit about the electrical short,' asked Barbie from the corner of her mouth.

'Not for a second,' I replied, smiling, and making it look like we had no concerns. Whoever the saboteur turned out to be, their latest stunt would be the memory that stuck in people's minds more than anywhere they went or anything they did.

Commander Yusef was doing the rounds with a pair of other senior officers. Their task to calm the crowd no doubt being repeated all over the ship while elsewhere the engineers frantically attempted to work out how the saboteur accessed the address system. Alistair would want answers and he would want them now. The familiar tug of a mystery to solve had the hem of my mental skirt and was becoming impossible to resist. Would I be able to sleep tonight if I didn't muck in to help out? What might the saboteur do next? What was the ultimate goal? These questions and more were swirling in a torrent around my skull, building momentum until they washed over me, and I swore quietly to myself.

Not as quietly as I thought though, 'Patty, are you okay?' asked Barbie, giving me side eye for my expletive.

I huffed out a breath. 'I've only been on board a few hours and there's already been a murder. Did you know there hasn't been so much as an accidental death since I left?'

She skewed her lips to one side, unable to work out what the correct response to my question might be. I was feeling sorry for myself and with no good reason. I wasn't the one lying in the morgue and I wasn't responsible for putting him there. In the end, Barbie went with, 'Do you think this could be the Godmother?'

Until that point, I hadn't considered it. Now I didn't know what to think. Was she that much more clever than I wanted to believe? I figured she would catch up to me on the ship at some point; my plan depended on it in many ways, but if this was her, then she arrived before me. Thinking it through, I shook my head. 'No, I don't think so. She wants me dead. I don't think she cares about anyone else and would only target you or Jermaine or even Sam to get to me. Creating panic on this ship achieves very little unless it is part of some bigger scheme I cannot perceive.'

Barbie said, 'We should get Sam back to his parents.'

She was right. Melissa was probably having kittens even though she knew her son was with me. There was still a crowd near the entrance but not so thick that it prevented people getting in and out. With Barbie leading the way, and my brain still whirling from the latest mystery to fall at my feet, we made our way back to Sam's cabin.

'Oh, thank goodness!' blurted a relieved mum as we came into view. She was wise enough to stay in one spot but too nervous to stay inside her suite. She was in the passageway, biting her nails and looking up and down on her tip toes to see over heads. When she saw us, we got to see the relief wash over her face.

'Hi, Mum,' said Sam, completely unaffected by the drama unfolding on board the ship. 'I had two pina coladas!' he announced.

Melissa pulled him into a quick hug before directing him inside to his dad so she could talk to me outside in the passageway. 'Do you know what just happened?' she asked, making it clear she not only hoped I had the inside line on the false tannoy announcement, but also showing that she trusted my opinion above that of any strangers, even if they were crew.

'Not really,' I shrugged. I didn't want to tell her there was a saboteur on board. Alistair would want no one to know because then the word couldn't spread. 'I think it was most likely what the captain said and just an electrical fault.'

Melissa accepted my answer at face value, used one arm to pull me into a hug and said, 'Thank you for taking care of him and bringing him back to me.'

'He took just as much care of me,' I told her. 'He held my hand and kept me safe. You should get to one of the bars for some food while the free stuff is still going. Grab Sam and head to La Trevita on deck fourteen. It's a wonderful Italian place. They have the area outside set up like a square in an Italian city.' I was going over the top to sell her the idea because it would do them good to get out and explore. Surely nothing else would happen tonight.

I hoped.

Bowels of the Ship

'You are certain?' he repeated for the third time.

'Yes, boss. They made a big song and dance of it. Harry and I both had to attend along with about three hundred others. The captain had us all congregate inside and then told us a special guest was coming on board. We were to treat the guests about to arrive as royalty and clap enthusiastically when their cars arrived and continue clapping until they got on the ship.'

Still sceptical because the news was simply too good to be true, Edward Smith, as he insisted they call him, moved to the wall where several pictures were arranged. It was his revenge mountain; one he planned to climb all the way to the top, killing each of the people in the pictures along the way. Snatching the highest picture, the one which would be the star if this were some kind of twisted Christmas tree, he yanked it free, sending the pushpin tumbling to the deck. 'Her,' he demanded, shoving the picture in the face of his two lackeys. 'This woman here is the one you saw coming on board today?'

Nicholai shrugged, unsure how he could say it any differently from the dozen ways he had already said it. 'Yes, boss. One hundred percent. She fell over getting out of the car. She got all twisted in the dog leads and showed the world her panties. They had to pick her up.'

A hard breath escaped Smith's nose as he turned the picture around to glare at it himself. Harry and Nicholai were the best he could hope for. They knew him, they knew what he was capable of and he had dirt on each of them. He'd never exposed their dirty secrets, so they owed him and that had got his foot in the door. Then he offered to make them rich, and he knew they would take the bait. Once they let him in, it was too late for either to back away without exposing themselves to criminal charges. His plan involved them up to a point and they would serve a glorious purpose as he got the vengeance he so rightly deserved.

'Patricia Fisher,' he murmured, chuckling to himself in a way that Harry and Nicholai thought was a little deranged. The world had turned to place her exactly where he needed her to be. He couldn't have asked for more.

Or could he?

As he put her picture back where it had come from, selecting a fresh pushpin to stick it to the wall, his eyes were drawn to the three pictures on the next tier. Alistair Huntley occupied the leftmost spot, but he pointed now to the other two.

'Were they with her?' he asked, his voice a surly growl.

Harry nodded his head vigorously, hoping they would be able to escape soon. Their boss was borderline crazy in his opinion and the scars on his face were both fresh and terrible to look at.

Nicholai answered, his Russian accent lilting his words. 'The hot blonde and the big black guy? Yes, boss, they were both with her. And another guy. White guy, big. Not as big as the black guy but he looked … I don't know how you would say it in English. Tough, maybe,' Nicholai hazarded. 'He looked like he could handle himself.'

'And there was a young woman. A small one,' reported Harry, suddenly remembering the last person to exit the car. 'Maybe that's her daughter?' he suggested with a wild guess.

Their boss snapped his head around to stare at them. 'A daughter? How old was she?'

Unexpectedly on the spot again, both men exchanged a hopeless glance. 'Maybe in her teens still?' Harry tried. 'Not a child, though she is quite short and petite.'

With a slowly exhaled breath, the man with the fake name closed his eyes and thought for a moment. His thoughts were delicious. He wanted revenge. He had no idea it could taste this good and perhaps the girl was to be the cherry on top. He could already envisage a perfect way to use her. Patricia Fisher's arrival on board the Aurelia was unexpected, and it changed the plan in many ways. For a start, there was no longer any need to get off the ship in England. It wasn't due to arrive there for many weeks, and every day he spent on board was another day when he could get caught. Being able to step up the plan and kill Patricia Fisher at the same time was the sweetest gift. He would have to work fast though, there were still systems on the ship he had yet to access.

Snapping his eyes open, he said, 'Bring her to me.' The request was calmly delivered in a conversational tone, but the two men had no doubt that it was an order. When neither moved, it only took a flaring of their boss's nostrils to make them scurry from his sight.

Left alone again, he rejoiced in the manner in which his plan was unfolding. Alistair Huntley had no idea what was to come. What had gone before was nothing. The real vengeance was about to begin. First, he had to take his biggest risk. He needed to retrieve something from the bridge.

It had been there for almost six months, hidden and undetected because no one knew to look for it. No one knew it existed except him. He felt like laughing.

Now that Sam was safely back with his parents, I couldn't decide what to do next. I felt I ought to check on Jermaine and Molly; especially Molly given the dire panic of half an hour ago, but I also wanted to find someone I knew from the security detail; I had questions and knew that if I asked the right person, I would get answers.

'Did you speak to Deepa yet?' I asked Barbie. Deepa Bhukari was arguably Barbie's best friend on board the Aurelia. Best female friend anyway since Barbie and Jermaine were as close as two people could get without a physical relationship. Her feelings for him were much the same as mine. Deepa was from Pakistan originally, but had left her birth country with her parents when aged nine and grew up in England thereafter. She spoke five languages fluently – most of the crew were multilingual – and had spent two years in the British Army before leaving because they would never let her fight on the front line no matter how good she was. Deepa was also beautiful and tough and had saved my life twice at least that I knew of.

Barbie shook her head. 'Not yet. There's always a lot for the security team to do when the ship sets off. The hours running up to leaving quayside, and the few hours that follow, are their busiest time, and then a body was found so that would have eaten up more resources, stretching the team even thinner. I didn't trouble her yet. When I spoke to her on the dock, she said she would come by later when she got a chance. She knows how to find me and still has my number.'

'Have you spoken to Jermaine?' I asked next. We were making our way back to my suite because I had barely spoken to him since we arrived, and he tended to fret. Agent Garrett tailed along behind us, quiet as always.

'Not since I left to take Molly to the pool,' replied Barbie.

I questioned, yet again, my decision to bring the young woman along with me. Would I be putting her in harm's way here or saving her from the clutches of the Godmother while simultaneously giving her the trip of a lifetime? 'I hope she's alright,' I murmured.

Barbie snorted a laugh. 'When I left her, she was eyeing up two boys on a pair of loungers across from her. She asked if it was allowed for her to sunbathe topless. The only thing you need to worry about with that one, is returning her home with an unwanted pregnancy.'

'Oh, goodness.' I hadn't considered that. She was a young woman away from home for the first time and surrounded by all manner of temptation. Modern values and morals seemed vastly different from when I was growing up.

I put it to one side as I fished in my bag for my door card.

'Here,' said Barbie, producing hers. 'I have one too this time around,' she chuckled. Last time we were on board, she was the gym instructor in the upper deck gymnasium. Now she was a guest. We all were, although Jermaine was somehow happier to be back in his old job.

'Jermaine, sweetie. Are you there?' I called as I slipped off my shoes. Just like before, my slippers were positioned next to the door for my use upon return. I knew better than to bend down to pick them up though. The stampeding noise of eight tiny paws preceded my miniature dachshunds skidding to a stop by my feet. Had I bent over to pick up my footwear, they would both have leapt at my face, attempting to impart their affection for me in a way only an excited dog can manage.

I scooped them both for kisses, getting my neck and chin licked in return.

'Madam,' said Jermaine, appearing just inside the central hub of my suite as if he had been waiting there like a silent sentinel since I left. It was a spooky trick of his to always know, somehow, that I was about to come back through the door. The first couple of months on board he kept making me jump, but after I swiped at his arm a hundred times, I learned to expect it.

'Is Molly here?' I asked.

'No, madam,' he replied, stepping out of the way so Barbie and I could get inside.

I wriggled my lips around as I tried to decide if I should worry about her absence. Most likely, she was still by the pool and chatting with boys. She might have made a friend or friends her own age; there had to be other teenage girls on board with their parents, and she had both a keycard to get back in and a swipe card to buy drinks or food or other items she might need.

A knock at the door just as we were moving into the central area of the suite, broke my train of thought. Barbie was closest to the door, but her sentence, 'I'll get it,' drove Jermaine to spring forward.

'Don't you dare,' he growled. She was playing with him, of course, teasing because she knew he felt it was his task to both greet and see guests out. This was the ship's royal suite after all.

I chuckled at their interplay; two friends who were comfortable teasing one another, and I paused to see who it might be. Jermaine stepped aside to let the visitors in, white uniforms appearing, and I thought for a moment it might be Alistair.

It wasn't though, it was Lieutenants Baker and Schneider, doffing their hats as they came inside.

'Mrs Fisher,' they each said once Jermaine had announced them. Then they both nodded their heads at Barbie, 'Barbie.'

'Hey, guys,' said Barbie, moving in to greet each with a hug. Martin Baker got a kiss on his cheek too, 'I'm so pleased for you,' Barbie gushed. 'I'm sure you will make Deepa a very happy woman. You are going to have to tell me all about the proposal later. I'll just get it from Deepa if you don't.'

Lieutenant Baker blushed but swung his focus back to me. 'We're here to see Mrs Fisher, of course,' he let us all know.

I knew why they were here. 'Come to enlist my help, have you, gentlemen?'

They had awkward expressions like they'd just been caught doing something naughty. Schneider said, 'Well, when you appeared below decks to see the body, we just kind of figured …' he trailed off.

'We hoped maybe you were getting involved again. There hasn't been a murder since you left the ship, you see?' said Baker.

I rolled my eyes. 'Patricia Fisher trouble magnet. Back on board for a few hours and the morgue is already beginning to fill.'

Schneider gave his colleague a nudge with his elbow and flared his eyes. 'Way to go, Baker.'

I flapped my arm at him. 'It's fine. I could tell poor Edgar was killed before I came on board. It just … it feels like old times, but not in a good way. It would be nice if people would stop getting murdered when I am on board.' I sighed. I already knew I was going to get involved. What else could I do? 'I think you should take me back to the start. Where did this saboteur strike first?'

Sabotage

Leaving the suite this time, I took the dachshunds with me. They needed some exercise though Jermaine assured me they had used the indoor doggy loo to do their business already. He elected to come with me, even though Wayne was with me for protection. I think he wasn't happy with having me out of his sight when he was used to being my bodyguard.

Barbie came too, at my side and ready to help because she said we were all in this together again. It felt like we were a sleuthing team from a television series. *Charlie's Angels* or something, only a new version for the twenty-first century with a tall gay black guy and a straight white guy alongside the blonde bombshell. However, I worried that in the scenario I just created, I was Bosley, the older man with little purpose.

Baker and Schneider led us down to the crew levels. Through winding passageways we meandered, the dogs tugging me along as they followed the people in front. They didn't know where they were going, but that didn't matter to them, they were in a hurry to get there no matter what.

'The first incident we can tie directly to a saboteur was twelve days ago,' explained Schneider, his Austrian accent reminding me, as always, of a famous bodybuilder turned actor. 'There were other things that happened before that which could have been him or her at work or might just have been unfortunate accidents.'

'Like what?' asked Barbie.

'Well the first one I want to show you is a forklift truck. Someone rewired the fail-safe, at least that's what the mechanics claim. Forklifts have a fail-safe that prevents them being started in gear. This one had been bypassed and then left in gear, which the driver swore he has never done in his life. Of course, he could have just forgotten, a distraction makes him forget and he thinks he has. He couldn't have accidentally rewired it though. The next watch takes over and the driver gets in to move food on pallets to the freight elevator, but the truck is in gear and shunts forward, knocking over a four-metre-high load. It looked like nothing – human error – until the mechanics gave it a check over and found the wiring had been tampered with.'

I had a question. 'You said there were other things before that might have been accidents but could have been the saboteur.' Actually, it wasn't a question, it was a prompt, but they got the idea.

Baker answered. 'Tampering with food might be the first thing.'

'All of the refrigerators were turned off,' explained Schneider. 'And I mean all of them. That's a lot of refrigerators. It makes me think it's a team.'

Baker sighed. 'There you go again with your conspiracy theory. There's no way there is a team doing this. It's got to be one person. One person with a grudge about something.'

Schneider looked down at his shorter teammate. 'One person cannot switch off that many refrigerators. It would take too long.'

'It could be done centrally, using the ship's onboard computer system. Everything can be controlled from there.'

'But's that on the bridge,' Schneider continued to argue. 'No one could tap into it undetected.'

'The chefs went nuts,' Baker told us, wisely dropping the distracting argument with his colleague. 'So much food was ruined, and we were two days from port. They had to get inventive with the meals and they ran out of lobster, which did not go down well with the passengers.'

I nodded my head, imagining how that news might be taken by people who would have spent a lot of money to be on board. No matter what one's budget, all, apart from the superrich, feel a cruise is an expensive luxury and they wouldn't want to hear that they needed to make compromises.

'That is the very first incident we are aware of,' Schneider told us. 'At the time it was dismissed. Questions were raised, of course, and the captain got an earful from the head chef who believes he is far more important than the man who runs the ship.'

Baker turned a corner, leading us starboard and walking backward for a moment while he talked. 'There's no point showing you that though. It's just switches, and like I said, there are too many for a single person to flick.'

'What do you want to show us?' asked Jermaine, voicing the curiosity I felt.

'Barbie!' The call, which came from a side passage, interrupted whatever Lieutenant Baker was about to say and running feet told us someone was coming our way at speed. Our party ground to a halt as Barbie backtracked to see who it was.

Drawing level with the adjoining passage again, she threw her arms in the air and squealed, 'Arrrgh!'

Agent Garrett's hand was immediately on the grip of his pistol. However, it was excitement, not terror, fuelling her scream as, moments later, two of her friends from the gym bounced into view. A woman and a man, both wearing Lycra and sporting more muscle than I thought was decent, wrapped Barbie into a three-way hug.

They all started talking at once, her friends asking if she was back for good, and Barbie asking what she had missed. I called out to her.

'Barbie, we're going to push on. You should stay here and catch up. We'll come back for you.'

'Okay,' she gave me a thumbs up and a swift smile.

Baker and Schneider set off again, turning yet another corner. I was thoroughly lost, the passageways down in the crew area all looked the same to me. They were labelled with an alpha numerical code which I'm sure the crew learn swiftly enough, but it bewildered me. We were in the crew accommodation part of the ship; I knew that much. However, given that there were more than two thousand crew on board, it was no surprise that one passageway looked like any other.

A smile split Jermaine's face. 'This is where my cabin used to be.'

Baker frowned. 'I thought your cabin was attached to the royal suite.'

'It is,' agreed Jermaine. 'But when I first came on board, I worked in a cabaret act for a while.' I'd forgotten about my tall, muscular butler's drag act. Changing the subject, rather than let it distract us, Jermaine reminded them, 'You were going to tell us what it was that you wanted to show us.'

They didn't answer straight away, they stopped walking instead. Baker pointed to a door. 'This is the anomaly. We both think it is the work of the saboteur, but we can't work out why.'

They were standing either side of a door. It looked just like any other door, of which there were hundreds on either side of the long passageway that stretched into the distance on both sides. The one exception with this door were the scorch marks on it. Even without seeing inside, it looked like the scene of an inferno.

'Whose cabin is this?' I asked.

Schneider answered. 'A chef from Botswana called Isibaya Motene. She wasn't in the room when it was firebombed, mercifully.' He opened the door so we could look inside. It was a blackened shell. Nothing could have survived. 'It happened at three in the morning. Honestly, it was a miracle she wasn't killed, only surviving because she had chosen to spend the night in someone else's cabin.'

'Do you think this was racially motivated?' asked Jermaine.

Baker took off his hat and scratched his head. 'That's just it. There doesn't seem to be any motivation. Racism just doesn't exist on board, so we don't think it is that. The alarm was raised by another chef, a man called George Seward. That's his cabin next door,' he pointed to the door right next to the one with the scorch marks. The doors were arranged in pairs on each side, the cabin opening out into a wider, but still miniscule space, once inside. 'He reported that he heard something – a bottle smashing he thought – but he rolled over to go back to sleep, only getting up to investigate when he heard popping noises.'

Schneider took over. 'We think the popping noises were aerosol cans exploding. Isibaya had hairspray and such on her desk. George burnt his hand on her door handle and had to be taken to hospital when we made port. Thankfully, the fire was contained in her cabin and his burn was the worst injury sustained. The sound of glass smashing was a bottle. The arsonist forced the door open and threw a Molotov cocktail in.'

I had listened to their tale but didn't see how it fit with anything else. 'This seems personal,' I commented. 'The other attacks, the refrigerators, the fire alarm system, today's debacle with the address system, were all aimed at impacting the maximum amount of crew and passengers. This attack, unless the perpetrator believed the fire would spread, was targeting one person only. The intention had to be murder. What makes you think this could be the work of the saboteur?'

Put on the spot, both men shared a glance, waiting for the other to field the question. In the end, it was Baker who answered. 'Because it's a crime without motivation. That's what links it. The saboteur will have motivation driving them to do what they are doing; we just have no idea what it is. This is the same thing. It looks different, because it has targeted a seemingly innocent chef from Botswana, but we don't get crime on board the ship.'

Except when I am here, I thought to myself. 'When did this happen?' I asked.

'Twenty days ago,' Schneider reported. 'It was before the concept of a saboteur evolved. We think this was the first crime. We just don't know why.'

I skewed my lips to one side, staring at the door in puzzlement. Was this connected? Was it a massive red herring? Were the chaps unable to pinpoint the saboteur and their motivation because they were following false leads? When I looked back up at Baker and Schneider, they had hopeful expressions on their faces.

Baker said, 'So, what do you think, Mrs Fisher? Can you help us to figure this out before someone else gets hurt?'

I asked a question instead of answering theirs. 'Did you interview her partner? I assume she was in someone else's room for sex. Is there a scorned woman you might have missed? A third person in a love triangle who might harbour a deep-rooted grudge?'

They both shook their heads. 'They both came on board single,' Baker assured me. 'Her boyfriend is another chef, a man called Wadiwa Molosi. They met when they were being inducted into the ship's crew.'

I stared at the door again. There were too many potentials at the moment. A yawn split my face, reminding me how messed up my body clock was. 'I have to get some sleep,' I muttered when the yawn finally subsided. 'I'll do what I can to help, chaps. Whether the arson is connected or not, I wouldn't like to say. It feels like it is something separate, but my brain might function a little better with some sleep.'

Baker dipped his head. 'Of course, Mrs Fisher. We'll escort you back to your suite.'

'There's no need,' said Wayne, speaking for the first time in thirty minutes. 'Jermaine can get us there. Can't you, Jermaine?'

Jermaine raised his eyebrows, but said, 'Of course.'

Wayne had a question. 'Just out of curiosity? Which of these cabins was yours?' His question gave me cause to pause. Not because of the question itself, but the way in which it was asked. To me, it seemed like Wayne was flirting. Some people talk about having a gaydar – the ability to determine the sexual orientation of men and women without needing to ask them. I don't have that. Or if I do, it is broken. Yet, the sly smile, when Wayne posed his question, would be out of place, unless his intention was to flirt with my butler.

I expected Jermaine to point his arm in one direction or the other, indicating that his cabin was one we passed earlier, or still to be reached, but he turned to point at the door behind him. 'It was this one.'

It was directly opposite the one which had been firebombed and I got a little itchy feeling at the back of my skull.

Missing Molly

On our way back to the suite, I suggested the girls ought to get a little fresh air. I planned to walk them outside for a while, because I didn't think it fair to keep them indoors the whole time, even if I did have an expensive and clever indoor doggy toilet.

'I think you may find it a little chilly outside, madam,' advised Jermaine. 'The temperature in these waters at night, at this time of year, is rarely above freezing. Perhaps we should return to your suite where we can don winter coats first.'

'The balcony of the suite might be a better destination too,' Wayne chipped in. When I looked at him, he held up his hands defensively. 'I know you think you are safe from the Godmother here, and you probably are. It is my job to keep you out of harm's way, which for me, means minimising exposure. Especially at night.'

I didn't like it, but I didn't wish to argue with him every time he tried to protect me. 'The sun terrace it is.' He cocked his head, not following my remark.

'Madam's suite has a sun terrace, not a balcony,' Jermaine explained.

Wayne frowned. 'What's the difference?'

'Size, mostly,' I said, to end the conversation. 'Let's get back to the suite.'

By my feet, Anna barked, which made Georgie bark, and then both dogs were barking and pulling at their lead. We'd made it back to the top deck already and were heading back to my suite along the galleried passageways that provide a view down to some of the decks below. They form the heart of the ship with shops, pools, restaurants, and bars spread out over many levels. There were plenty of passengers and crew about, it was still only mid-evening, and I couldn't work out what was making the girls bark until a little sausage dog burst through the legs of a man trying desperately to get out of the way.

It was a cute dappled black and tan with one piecing light blue eye. He was leaning into his collar and trying to bound forward while being held back by the person holding his lead. That person was the lady from the bar, the one who thought I was royalty.

Knowing it would be rude to hurry on my way, even though I was tired and all I wanted to do was get back to my suite for some sleep, I turned her way and followed my own dachshunds as they pulled me to meet the new dog.

'Calm down, girls,' I begged, feeling my feet being tugged forward by their excitement. They didn't get to see many dogs. At home I tended to walk them in the woods that sit inside the boundary of my property. When we do go out, seeing another dachshund is a rarity. In fact, now that I thought about it, the only ones I have ever seen in England are Tempest Michaels'.

Perhaps that was what had made them so keen to meet this one and for a heartbeat, I questioned whether Anna might be in season again. She couldn't be though. It was a once every six months thing and Georgie was only ten weeks old now.

'Hello,' I waved to the woman from the bar. She was almost out of control as her dog made a badly behaved beeline for the dogs he could see.

'No, Rufus!' she yelled at him. 'No. Bad dog!' Rufus wasn't listening and he had enough momentum to keep tugging her along.

To help her, before she fell over, I moved in her direction, closing the distance until the dogs met and the tension in Rufus's lead slackened.

The poor woman was out of breath, so while she got her breathing under control, I did the talking. 'What a sweet little dog you have. It's a boy, yes?' Rufus was sniffing where a dog sniffs, but then so too were Anna and Georgie, all three dogs climbing over each other to make their leads into a bag of snakes.

'Yes, he's a boy,' she wheezed. 'A very naughty boy. Why didn't you listen, Rufus?' She looked genuinely angry with her tiny sausage dog but met my eyes and smiled. 'He is such a little pickle. I've tried training him, but he just does what he wants.'

I pulled an oops face. 'They are known for being headstrong, apparently. I had a devil of a time getting Anna to stop biting people. I think it will be easier with the puppy, Georgie, because I get to train her from birth.'

'You didn't have Anna as a puppy?' the lady enquired. Then she blushed. 'Sorry, I haven't introduced myself. I'm Verity Tuppence. I'm from Weston-Super-Mare in Somerset. This is my first time on a cruise. I'm so sorry about earlier. Isn't it funny that we should meet like this and both have little dachshunds with us? Is this your butler?' She was gabbling nervously, words spewing from her mouth in a torrent.

Quite what might be causing her nervousness, I couldn't imagine. We were of similar age and from the same country. Was it the two men flanking me that put her on edge? I smiled in a bid to settle her. 'I'm Patricia Fisher,' I reminded her since I'd already announced myself earlier in the bar.

'Oh, I know!' Verity exclaimed. 'I knew I knew your name from somewhere, so I did a little research. When I looked up Patricia Fisher on the internet, I found you and got to read all about your exploits. It was truly amazing: the thing you did in Zangrabar. What an amazing life you have led.' She was gabbling again, her mouth running away with itself.

'There's nothing particularly special or amazing about me,' I assured her. 'I'm from a little village in Kent. This is Jermaine, my butler,' I indicated the man dressed in full ship's livery with tails and white gloves. 'And this is Wayne Garrett.' I didn't explain that he was a police officer assigned to be my bodyguard, it would just raise too many questions. Another yawn split my features and I had to turn away when I couldn't wrestle it under control. 'I'm terribly sorry,' I chuckled when it finally died. 'I flew in from the UK to meet the ship here today and my body-clock is a little discombobulated. I really must get some sleep. It was lovely meeting you.'

'And you,' she replied quickly as I started to move away.

I tugged at the girls' leads. 'Come along, ladies. Mummy needs some shut eye.' And maybe another gin to make sure I sleep, I added inside my head. I hadn't eaten yet and there was still the offer of a nightcap with Alistair. I would have something to shut my stomach up, but it couldn't be anything heavy or I would suffer indigestion and get no sleep.

'See you again?' called Verity loudly.

I waved, rather than reply. I would be friendly, but I wasn't here to make friends. I made plenty on the last trip, none of whom I had much hope of ever seeing again. Bumping into Rick and Akamu in London had been a joy, but not one I expected to ever get to repeat. I would see Lady Mary on occasions when our diaries aligned, but I didn't want to make more friends who would touch my life and then vanish from it.

Finally back at my suite, I slipped off my shoes while Jermaine opened the door. Wayne went in first, his right hand inside his jacket so it was close to the grip of his gun as he checked through the rooms. I felt he was being overly cautious but could also name half a dozen times when people who shouldn't have been able to get into my suite had miraculously appeared there. There had even been a murder in my kitchen, right back at the start of my adventure.

Once free of their collars, the girls gambolled about, chasing each other and rolling on their backs to ruffle their own fur. By the time I got to the kitchen, where Jermaine proposed to make me a light snack, the dogs were on a couch and curling into balls.

Barbie came through the suite's main entrance door before I could get my bottom onto one of the breakfast-bar stools and she had Deepa Bhukari with her.

The dogs were up again instantly, barking to repel the intruders until the two women scooped the dogs up and into their arms, thus defeating the terrible sausage attack with affection.

'Oh, my goodness,' squealed Deepa, holding Georgie aloft. 'She is so tiny. I could fit her in my pocket.'

'You could fit her in your cleavage,' joked Barbie which caused Deepa to play act as if she were going to lower the dog into her top. Deepa was off duty, dressed down in jeans, heels and a cotton top. It was warm on the ship, the temperature outside having no effect on our environment. It made me reconsider my idea to take the dogs onto the sun terrace since that would flood the room with cold air.

'Hi, Patricia,' said Deepa, coming across to air kiss me with Georgie balanced in one hand. 'It's so nice to see you again.'

'Likewise,' I smiled. 'Now, where is the rock Barbie told me about?'

The next few minutes were absorbed with chat about her diamond engagement ring and the coming nuptials. They were to get married on the upper deck of the ship in just two weeks' time. They wanted it done on board and were flying in some family to join them. Alistair would perform the ceremony on the upper deck with the guests getting an incredible view.

Yawning again, I announced my intention to retire to bed and downed the last of my gin. It was only at that precise moment that I spotted what was amiss. 'Where's Molly?'

Search

Deepa's obvious question of, 'Who's Molly?' got a swift explanation from Barbie. It was almost ten o'clock which meant that, apart from a few hours of sleep on the plane from London to Montreal, none of us had slept in over thirty hours. Molly hadn't slept on the flight either, too excited to be on a plane and flying first class to miss any of it.

One phone call was all it took to have Baker and Schneider standing in my suite. 'You said you left her chatting with some other teenagers,' Baker tried to confirm.

Barbie shook her head. 'No. I said there were other teenagers there and she was eyeing up a pair of boys. She might have plucked up the courage to talk to them, or accidentally on purpose bumped into one of them at the bar. I'm going to head back down to the pool just in case she fell asleep on the lounger and is still there.'

Deepa grabbed her purse. 'I'll go with you.'

'They close the pools at nine o'clock,' Baker reminded everyone. 'The lifeguards will have asked her to move on and will have woken her if she was asleep.'

Deepa shrugged. 'It's still worth making sure she isn't in that area. I'll check who the on-duty lifeguards were this evening and see if anyone remembers her.' She was thinking clearly, which was more than I could say of myself. My brain felt like it was coated in fog. Barbie had to be just as tired as me but there was no sign of her fatigue and it was probably to do with the four gin and tonics in my blood compared to just one in hers which was probably metabolised by now.

They darted from the suite, moving swiftly, but almost colliding with someone else arriving outside. It was Alistair, my proposed nightcap with him completely forgotten in the events of the evening.

Baker and Schneider stood a little more stiffly as their captain entered my suite, rapping his knuckles on the door on the way in. 'Good evening. Am I disturbing something?'

'My youngest charge is missing,' I told him, rising from the couch much to the disgruntlement of the dogs. As they grumped their displeasure and settled into the warm spot I left behind, I added, 'It's most likely nothing. She's not a child, but she isn't answering her phone and none of us have seen her in hours. Chances are she is with friends, but I am not inclined to leave things to chance anymore.'

Getting a sense for the concern I was trying to hide, Alistair acted. 'Baker, scramble B shift. I want Mrs Fisher's missing party member found as soon as possible. Do you want her returned here, Patricia?' he asked my opinion.

'No. She's a grown woman. If she is with a man or with some friends in one of the bars or clubs, she has every right to her freedom. I wish to know where she is though. She left here in a very skimpy bikini many hours ago and had only a towel to cover herself. Since swimwear isn't allowed in any of the bars and restaurants, except those around the pools which are now closed, I don't see how she can be in one of them.'

'What about the address system, sir?' asked Schneider, just as Baker was moving toward the door to perform his task. 'It has been used before to find lost children.'

Baker paused. 'That's right, sir. It could circumvent a lot of manhours searching deck by deck across the ship.'

Alistair gave the suggestion some thought. 'That's good thinking. Well done, Schneider. Report to Commander Yusef on the bridge. Have him make the announcement himself, but in a manner that will not cause alarm. Have him ask her to identify herself to any member of crew. If she isn't found swiftly, we will know we might have a bigger problem.'

'Very good, sir.' Schneider hurried toward the door.

Baker asked, 'And B shift, sir?'

'Not yet. Rouse them if there is no response to the announcement. I will re-join you on the bridge soon.'

Both men ran from the suite, leaving Alistair and I alone. Well, alone if one doesn't count my bodyguard and butler. Thankfully, it only took a moment for them to realise they were unnecessary, Wayne making an excuse about needing sleep but pausing to beg that I not attempt to leave the suite without him at my side.

I stated that I planned to remain where I was until Molly was found and bade him a good night.

'Nightcap?' asked Alistair.

I was bone tired, but I could hardly curl up in my bed when Molly might conceivably be in trouble. I also couldn't have any more to drink, not without affecting my ability to do anything else. The last thing I needed while alone with my former lover, was impaired decision making.

'Perhaps a coffee,' I suggested. 'A strong one.'

Alistair took off his jacket. 'That would be better.' We moved to the kitchen where he went about the process of making coffee. The suite's kitchen was well-appointed with high-end gadgets, not least of which was the kind of coffee machine one might more typically find a barista operating. Nevertheless, Alistair had no trouble getting it to produce two cups of thick, dark espresso.

'This should reinvigorate you,' he said as he passed me a small white porcelain cup.

As my fingers closed around it, the address system beeped, and the dulcet tones of the Turkish deputy captain came through a speaker set into the wall of my suite. The speakers were in every cabin and suite. They were everywhere on the ship and would cut over the beating disco beat in the clubs, and the background music in the restaurants.

'Good evening ladies and gentlemen. This is Deputy Captain Yusef speaking. I apologise for interrupting your evening, but I have an important message to pass to one person. Can Molly Lawrie please identify herself to any member of crew.' He repeated the message, but it didn't go out in any other languages as a public announcement usually would – their target was English.

I drank my coffee. 'That ought to do it.'

Alistair put a hand on my arm. 'Let's hope she heard it and has the good sense to respond swiftly.' He kept his hand on my arm and I liked the warmth of it. It reminded me of his gentle touch and how much he thrilled me when we'd slept together. Was I ready for that again? I bit my lip, wondering if I should just give in and see what happened if I followed my feelings for once instead of letting my head rule.

Just as I was about to say something that would open the door for him to walk back into my life, he lifted his hand and stood up. 'I ought to return to the bridge. My shift ended an hour ago, but there is much to do. I have a crew working on the address system, trying to work out how and where the saboteur accessed it, and how to prevent it from happening again. I shall make sure that you are informed the moment Miss Lawrie is found.'

He slipped his jacket back on as I got to my feet to see him out. I thought he might try to kiss me at the door, but he barely paused to say goodnight as if he were trying to get away before I could attempt to kiss him. It left me feeling rejected, and at the same time aware that the emotion I now felt might have been his aim. If so, it was clever on his part. Slightly manipulative, but clever nonetheless, because now that he'd dangled the bait and snatched it away, I wanted to take it. Up until right now, I had felt ambivalent.

Knowing the right thing to do was wait in the suite until Molly was found or returned of her own accord, I settled onto the couch and fell promptly asleep.

Murder Most Unexpected

I awoke to the sound of two tiny dogs barking. Dachshunds have deceptive barks. They are small dogs, but they don't yip, not even as puppies. They have a bark that, on the other side of a closed door, would make a person expect a dog five times the size. The sudden and loud sound startled me, so too the lights flicking on around me.

Blearily, I pulled my face away from the material of the couch where it was almost stuck with drool. I'd fallen asleep sitting up with the two dogs on either side of me but slumped over in my sleep until my head came to rest on the arm. Voices told me people were already in the room, but I was shocked to see Deepa and Barbie approaching me with tears streaming down their faces.

My heart stopped beating. They were about to tell me Molly's body had been found. I'd brought the teenage housemaid away to keep her safe and yet she'd been murdered within hours of coming on board. It had to be the work of the Godmother. Who else could strike so quickly and so clinically, picking off the one member of my party who was out by herself?

My throat began to swell as the pain of loss, and regret for bringing the poor girl into my problems, overwhelmed me.

'It's Commander Yusef,' blurted Barbie. 'He's been murdered!'

A torrent of mixed emotions tore at me. Relief that it wasn't Molly's death they were here to report after all, horror that anyone had been killed, fear for what this might mean, and sorrow for the man and for his family for I knew he had a wife and children somewhere.

All I could manage to say in response was, 'Commander Yusef?'

'Yes,' said Deepa, tears making a mess of her makeup. 'He's just been found in his private quarters. He was stabbed through the heart.' Her voice was breaking as she sobbed. Commander Yusef was a kindly man who was liked by everyone. Stabbed through the heart was no accident and it made it two murders in a twenty-four-hour period.

'Any news of Molly?' I asked, certain there wouldn't have been but desperate to have it confirmed.

Both women shook their heads, a sprinkling of tears falling as they dislodged them from their eyelashes.

I was off the couch and my brain was coming up to speed. My phone, which I'd left on a side table showed me the time: it was quarter to four in the morning. Molly had been missing for twelve hours. Possibly less than that, depending on when she disappeared from the pool, but I had to accept that she might very well have been taken by someone. She must have heard the announcement made by Commander Yusef, and if not, because perhaps she had fallen asleep, then the people she was with would have heard it. The only conclusion I could draw was that she was being held against her will. That was one problem, but I set it aside because I was sure the security team were hard at work trying to find her.

The more immediate questions I had were to do with Commander Yusef and how he came to be murdered in his private quarters. 'His cabin is on the bridge level, isn't it? Same as the captain's.'

Deepa nodded, taking a tissue from a box offered by Barbie so she could blow her nose and wipe her eyes. 'Yes. It means he could only have been killed by one of the crew,' she sobbed.

I narrowed my eyes, but not at her. I was squinting at the mystery I faced. Two murders in the space of a day. Molly was missing, there was a saboteur on board, and a cabin belonging to a chef from Botswana had been firebombed. How many of those parts were linked to each other? It felt like I had to put together a jigsaw without a picture of what it was supposed to look like and a suspicion that the pieces in the box were from more than one puzzle.

One thing was for certain, I wasn't staying in the suite any longer. I needed to find Alistair, get special permission to visit the bridge and try to work out who would want to kill the deputy captain. His death had a note of determination to it. Edgar Thomas could have been the poor unfortunate who disturbed the saboteur and died from being in the wrong place at the wrong time. Not so Commander Yusef. Molly might not be kidnapped or dead, and the firebombing might be racially motivated; I might never know, but it took effort to get to Commander Yusef's cabin so that was the thread I would try to unravel.

The sound of a door opening caused the dogs to spin around and race toward the kitchen. Jermaine must have heard our voices because he was up and back in the suite. Dressed in light and dark blue vertically striped pyjamas and a matching dark blue silk robe with a teddy bear motif on the left breast pocket, he came through the kitchen, fielding my dogs deftly with his large hands.

He took one look at Barbie, his very good friend, and went to her, pulling her into a hug so her tears could dampen his shoulder.

I felt myself rising above it. A cool head was needed, it might as well be mine. 'Deepa,' I snapped to get her attention. 'What did you learn about Molly from the lifeguards? Did they remember seeing her? Was she with anyone when she left?'

The suddenness of my questions jolted her into answering. Blowing her nose again, and wiping her face, she pushed away her tears. 'None of them recognised the pictures we showed them.' They had a few shots from her social media profile to show around. 'The description of her string bikini didn't help either, the lifeguards say they see so many girls wearing next to nothing, they don't even notice anymore. If she left the pool with anyone, it wasn't seen by the crew on duty there.'

Another dead end.

I had more questions though. 'Have you spoken with Baker or Schneider in the last few hours? I believe they were coordinating whatever search effort was being put in place?'

Deepa took a shuddering breath as she brought herself back under control. Barbie detached herself from Jermaine so all three were paying attention. 'I last spoke to Mike around one o'clock. They were watching the crowds leaving the clubs and hoping to pick her up there. Obviously, if she has been taken by someone, finding her will be next to impossible, so they were focussing their efforts on the concept that she might have had a bit too much to drink and be unaware of the search for her. They haven't had any luck, I know that much, but I don't know what they are doing now. I would imagine they all got recalled by the captain when Commander Yusef's body was discovered.'

'How did you find out?' I asked her.

'Mike sent me a text message,' she replied quietly. 'He knew I would want to know. I wanted to go to the bridge, but it must be chaos up there at the moment. They won't want extra people getting in the way.'

Chaos. The word stuck in my head. Someone – the saboteur – was creating chaos. Was that the goal? Or was it a side effect of a different goal? What could the end goal be? Nothing the saboteur had done was permanent until now unless the goal was to ruin the vacation experience for the passengers. And if that were the case, then how did Commander Yusef's murder impact them? They wouldn't even learn of it.

Making a decision, I started toward my bedroom, a destination I intended to reach many hours ago and was yet to arrive at. 'They might not want extra people getting in the way, but they are going to have to put up with one more,' I announced with utter determination. I was going all in now. Someone was messing with the ship that I had come to love and think of as a second home. I returned because I believed I would be safe here for a while but in less than a day, one of us was missing, a man I knew had been killed, and I could not shift the feeling that I was somehow linked to the cause.

Whoever the saboteur was, whoever was behind Commander Yusef's death, and whoever had Molly, be they one person responsible for all three things or three separate people operating independently, I was going to track them down and make them pay.

The Bridge

With five hours sleep in the bag and a belly full of fire, I was ready to go again. In my bedroom, I found all my things laid out exactly as they were during my last time on board: Jermaine was a wonder to have around. I touched up my makeup, using a little extra to deal with the bags under my eyes, refreshed my perfume and deodorant and changed my clothes. It was five minutes of delay that I felt was necessary to avoid scaring people when I went outside. I really wanted a shower, but it would have to wait.

Coming back outside into the central area of the suite, I addressed Deepa first. 'Deepa can you get me onto the bridge?'

She looked stunned for a second, but then I got a one shoulder shrug as she thought about it. 'Sure, probably. I'll call through.'

'Speak to the captain,' I suggested. 'Or make sure the question about me is asked of the captain. If he doesn't want me involved, there's no point fighting it. However, I think it more likely that he will send an escort down to retrieve me when you ask the question.' As she moved aside to make a call, I looked at Barbie. She had been operating on caffeine, adrenalin, and pure will for hours. She still looked flawless, but now also dead tired. 'Barbie, you ought to get some sleep. I have no idea what the day ahead will bring. Even a couple of hours will help you.'

She knew I was right, but she still argued. 'I can help, Patty. I can …'

I raised a hand, begging her to stop. 'Not this time. You were running around in the search for Molly while I slept. We all need rest.' Dismissively, hoping that she would take the cue and go to bed, I looked away from her, effectively ending our conversation. 'Jermaine, sweetie, how are you feeling?'

'Refreshed, madam. I can be dressed for action in just a few minutes.'

'Very good. I think though that for now, you should also rest.' A sigh escaped my lips, followed by a sadly wry laugh. 'I expected to get a massage and relax. My plan was to eat well and exercise. I even brought a book with me. Now I have a feeling there isn't going to be much rest this week.' Snapping out of my funk before it got a chance to grip me, I looked around the room with a smile of fortitude. 'Molly has to be found, and Commander Yusef's killer brought to justice. I will be doing what I can to achieve those two things.'

'I spoke with Lieutenant Baker,' said Deepa, using her intended's formal rank and name. 'You will be met at the bridge elevator. They are expecting you.'

Nodding to myself, as I considered the scope of the task ahead, I thanked Deepa. 'You should get some sleep too. You must have a watch coming up soon.'

'In three hours,' she admitted wearily.

'I'm sorry it has been such a busy night. I will return shortly.'

Jermaine moved to intercept my path. 'Madam, surely you do not propose to make your way to the bridge alone. Should I wake Agent Garrett?'

I had completely forgotten my appointed bodyguard. Waking him to walk me the short distance to the bridge elevator felt like overkill. Yes, it was the middle of the night and the passageways would have their lights dimmed, but the ship would also be deserted as everyone on board, less essential crew, got some sleep.

'Let's leave him to sleep. It's not far,' I tried, knowing Jermaine would argue.

He flipped his eyebrows. 'I shall see you safely there, madam.' I knew there was no point in arguing. I expected to have to wait as he hurriedly dressed himself, but he simply walked to the door in his house slippers, pyjamas, and robe.

Barbie and Deepa air-kissed and went in different directions, Barbie to her room and Deepa to the door with Jermaine. Anna and Georgie looked at me from the couch, their chins resting on the edge of the seat, but they were eyeing me suspiciously rather than with interest. They wanted to go back to sleep and were worried I might be about to insist they come with me.

I left the lazy sausages to snooze and let Jermaine escort me to the bridge. Access to it was via an elevator which required a code and swipe card to open and operate. It wasn't normally guarded, but it came as no surprise to find two junior members of the security team stationed there now. If they felt a need to comment about Jermaine's pyjamas, they were wise enough to remain silent.

'Mrs Fisher?' the one on the left asked. She looked to be in her early twenties, with sparkling green eyes beneath hazel hair pulled straight and tucked into her hat. I couldn't tell if she was new and thus wasn't around when I was creating havoc last time or was one of those I never got to meet.

Her colleague, a man this time and slightly older, recognised me, 'Yes, this is Mrs Fisher.' He was smiling at least and hadn't said it with a groan.

I smiled and said, 'Morning,' leaving out the word, 'Good,' because there was little that ought to be celebrated on the way to see a dead man's body.

The woman spoke to someone via her radio, letting people above know we were coming up and the man operated the controls, punching in a code while using his body to ensure we couldn't see what it was. As the door closed, I realised Jermaine was still with me.

'I thought you were just escorting me to the bridge,' I pointed out.

Stiffly, he replied, 'I believe Wayne would prefer to know someone is with you since he is not, madam.'

The doors opened again just a few seconds later and we were on the bridge. Or to be more accurate, we were on the same level as the bridge. The pilot's seat, the navigation hub, the captain's arena from which he oversaw the ship and everything that happened onboard, was located in a superstructure close to the front of the ship. Set high above the top deck, the bridge occupied an area at the front of the superstructure.

A familiar face was there to greet us. 'Mrs Fisher,' said Lieutenant Baker with a nod to Jermaine. He looked both pleased to see me and exhausted from his day. I suspected his shifts had rolled from one to the next, the drama of having multiple problems to deal with too urgent to permit downtime.

There was nothing to be gained by mentioning it, so I simply said, 'Show me.'

I wasn't sure where the deputy captain's quarters were located but it turned out they were right next to the captain's, which seemed logical but also meant I had passed them dozens of times without noticing the title on the door. As expected, the route to his door was blocked by people. Crew, to be precise, and most of them in the white uniform of the security team. A gurney had been parked against the wall onto which they would load the body once it was ready to go.

Dr Kim's voice echoed out from inside the deputy captain's cabin. He would remember me, I felt certain. There were three doctors on board the Aurelia. They had sunburn and grazes to deal with mostly, but cruise ships attract a lot of retirement age travellers, keen for the slow pace of life a cruise ship offers, and heart attacks, strokes, and just plain old dropping dead were not uncommon. Then there were the rare, but not unheard of injuries from altercations, usually the result of alcohol and revealing swimsuits in combination, and the even rarer stabbings, strangulations, shootings, and other terrible injuries that I had been witness to during my three-month cruise.

Dr Kim took them all in his stride. The murmur of my arrival passing through the crew outside the cabin reached inside from where Alistair appeared. He looked chipper when I first saw him yesterday afternoon, and hopeful when he came to my suite before bed last night. Now he looked a little beaten. He would have been asleep and roused by his crew when they delivered the news. He was in his uniform, but his jacket was missing, and I could tell he'd dressed in a hurry.

I went to him, offering my hand for comfort. 'This is terrible, Alistair.'

He nodded his head sombrely. 'I cannot fathom who would have wanted to do this. He is popular with the crew, and well respected by them to my knowledge. He isn't the sort to be involved in some sordid love triangle that might have evoked a jealous ex-lover to a rage level sufficient to cause murder.'

He was walking as he talked, taking me inside the commander's cabin where Dr Kim knelt on the carpet. His back obscured my view of Commander Yusef but only until I moved into the room and stood to the side. I glanced behind me to find Jermaine had chosen to wait outside; the small cabin was already crowded.

The deputy captain lay on his back, his sightless eyes open to stare at the ceiling, or perhaps to the heavens as life seeped from him. Buried to the hilt in his chest was a knife; the handle protruding from his pristine white jacket looked like that of a regular kitchen knife.

'I shall have to call his wife,' Alistair murmured. 'What time is it in Turkey, please?' His question was aimed at anyone in the room or near vicinity, and he got his answer back from a dozen sources swiftly. 'I'll do it now,' he whispered in a distracted way, letting my hand go so he could depart, he was leaving me behind as if he expected me to now take over and find Yusef's killer.

He wasn't the only one it seemed, for when I turned to watch him leave the cabin, all the faces in the room were looking my way and so were most of the faces outside, expectant eyes peering into the cabin to see what I might say.

Since I had their audience, I narrowed my eyes and asked, 'Which one of you did it?' My question startled them, eyes flaring in shock as one or two jaws dropped. It also made them look at each other, glancing this way and that at the people around them, those standing to their left and right, as they wondered if they might be standing next to a killer. I gave it a two count before I added, 'Before you all start protesting your innocence, the bridge is the most secure place on this vessel. No one can access it without the code for the elevator and anyone arriving at the bridge level without knowing where they were going would be challenged instantly. How often do you get people up here by accident?'

I posed the question to no one in particular but my eyes were locked on Lieutenant Baker's, making him answer. 'Never,' he replied calmly. 'It's almost impossible to get to this level. The killer has to be a member of crew. No one else would be able to find their way to his cabin.'

'That's assuming he was the target,' said Schneider, which made the crowd swing their eyes his way.

'I need room,' announced Dr Kim, standing up. 'There're too many people in here now. I am finished, so the body can be moved unless you need it to remain here for investigation purposes.' He was looking at the security team for an answer, and they were looking at me.

I was looking at something else. Dr Kim had been obscuring my view of it with his body until he moved toward the door, and I wondered if anyone else had seen it. 'What's that?' I pointed under the built-in desk set against the opposite wall.

Around me, more than a dozen heads dipped to look where my arm pointed. The nearest officer, a young woman, crouched to look, then pulled the chair out of the way and crawled under the desk. There was a loose panel in the wall, which moved when she touched it. It hadn't been put back in properly, which was how I came to spot it.

The young woman reached forward, but half a dozen of her colleagues yelled for her to stop.

'We need to examine that for prints and take photographs before we touch it,' said Baker, the woman sliding back out with a red face at her mistake.

I sagged a little. 'I'm leaving the room. You are the security team and charged with conducting the investigation. I am trying to find my missing housemaid. Do I assume the search for her has been halted because of Commander Yusef?'

Baker looked guilty. 'Yes, Mrs Fisher. We are running out of places to look and we don't actually have a reason to believe anything has happened to her.'

'This is me we're talking about,' I pointed out as I left the cabin.

Schneider said, 'She's got a point there.'

Baker sniffed. 'It will be daylight in a few hours. We will resume the search then. Right now, we need to deal with Commander Yusef because Mrs Fisher is right: this is our job, not hers. I want pictures of his body, I want the door frame and handle checked for prints, I want …' his list went on for a while as he started doling out tasks to the eager team.

Had one of them killed the deputy captain?

Uniform

The man calling himself Edward Smith hadn't really wanted to kill Commander Yusef. Not that he really cared either way, and in the end, it would make no difference, not with what he had planned for the ship. He needed to retrieve the bag from the deputy captain's cabin, and he needed to steal a spare pair of dress uniform shoes and his hat. Had the man not walked in, he would still be alive. He sealed his own fate by choosing the wrong moment to return to his rooms. The man calling himself Edward Smith pushed thought of it from his mind and washed the blood from his hands. He needed them clean before he started work on the uniform. He probably could have found one that was his size, and then sewn the correct rank insignia on it, but there was something poetic about taking the captain's and adjusting the sleeves and trouser legs so it would fit his longer limbs.

The uniform wasn't essential to the plan. One might even suggest that it was silly. He wanted it for the final stage which happily he could now bring forward. Originally, he expected to remain hidden on board until the ship reached Southampton. It would make a two-day stop there which would be enough time for him to find and kill Patricia Fisher. Before her body was even cold, he would be safely back on the Aurelia where the British police would never find him. With that part of his revenge neatly ticked off, he could finish with his glorious final act. A romantically historic manoeuvre that would be televised around the globe and live on in history. They would remember his name, his real name, and they would know why he did it.

His steward's uniform had blood on the cuff, something he'd had to hide on his way back down from the bridge. He stripped the tunic off, discarding it into a corner - he wouldn't need it again – and stepped in front of a mirror to remove the makeup and prosthetics he'd employed to make himself less recognisable. Being recognised was the only danger and the very thing which had kept him below decks since he came on board. He would need to venture above decks again soon, the final act demanded it.

Harry and Nicholai were almost at the end of their usefulness, but he wasn't going to dispose of them just yet. There were one or two jobs they could still complete, one which they were already supposed to be doing, and he had an inkling he might need to use their deaths to lay a false trail. He'd followed Patricia Fisher's career with interest, surprised by her luck each time she manged to stumble over the solution to a mystery. He could visualise her now, sticking her busybody nose in and sniffing around. Maybe he would need to throw her off the scent. He had a plan for that too.

Sombre Moments

Alistair reappeared after making the call to Commander Yusef's wife. He was correctly dressed now, looking resplendent in his full uniform, but his face failed to hide the pain he felt. I could only imagine what it was like to break the news to his colleague's wife. He retreated to his own private quarters to do it, but now he had work to do. His security team would investigate, but Commander Yusef's death left him without a deputy. How could Alistair sleep if there was no one to take over his duties?

Of course, the rank system functioned to provide an immediate next in line and that person would have to be woken, informed, and then, as they stepped up to assume the deputy captain's duties, their own duties would fall to someone else. That would cascade downwards and outwards as the same amount of work had to be covered by fewer people until they made it to port and a new person could be brought on board.

'Who is next in line?' I asked him.

'Commander Ochi. He is the head of Engineering. I think he may refuse the post or, at least, wish to only fill it until we make port. Seniority dictates that he is next in line though, so it has to be offered to him first.' Changing subjects, he said, 'I understand the young lady you brought on board with you is missing?'

I huffed a breath out through my nose. 'That's right. She might have made new friends and be with them, she might have met a boy, or she might have been kidnapped. I'm telling myself it has to be the former, but you know why I came back, don't you?'

He nodded. 'When you explained about the Godmother and your need to return to the Aurelia, I thought you would be safe here. Do you think this could be her?'

'Molly going missing?' I pursed my lips. 'I just don't know. I don't see how the Godmother could have got her agents on board before me. How could they react that quickly? It would mean a breach in Scotland Yard because we didn't tell anyone, and we went from deciding, to packing, then leaving, in just a couple of days. But if she is being held against her will, who is behind it if it isn't the Godmother?'

Lieutenant Schneider appeared. We were at the rear of the bridge control room where Alistair was making sure all was in order and having all crew on watch check their areas thoroughly to report all-clear. The last thing he wanted was another act of sabotage to top off what had already happened. Turning to face his Lieutenant, he said, 'Report.'

Schneider made a face, unsure how to form his next sentence. 'Sir, I have something odd to report.'

Alistair tilted his head, looking at the younger man and wondering what he was about to say. 'Go on,' he encouraged.

'Earlier today there was a report from the crew laundry unit. I dismissed it as insignificant, given what was going on already.'

Alistair interrupted, 'You're being cryptic, Schneider, please get to the point.' He sounded calm yet irritated.

'Yes, sir. One of your uniforms was stolen.'

'Stolen?' I echoed, getting in before Alistair.

'That would appear to be the case,' Schneider agreed. 'I apologise, sir, this hasn't been followed up on yet.'

Alistair waved a dismissive hand. 'Everyone is working hard. It was definitely stolen?'

'According to the team in the laundry unit, but like I said, I haven't followed up on it yet.' Schneider looked embarrassed but he didn't need to be. There were saboteurs, and missing people and murders to deal with. A missing uniform that might turn out to be misplaced? It just wasn't going to make it onto the list of things to do.

'Let's just ignore it,' Alistair suggested. 'We have bigger fish to fry.'

'Yes, sir,' replied Schneider automatically, but his face couldn't hide that he had something else to say on the matter. 'Only ... it looks like there are items missing from Commander Yusef's wardrobe too.'

'Items of uniform?' Alistair tried to clarify.

'Yes, sir.'

'It is not being cleaned?' asked Jermaine.

Schneider sounded quite certain when he replied, 'No. That has been checked. His rooms have been thoroughly searched. We cannot find his hat, a pair of dress shoes appear to be missing, and a picture frame has been taken from his desk.'

'We only get one hat, but four dress uniforms,' Alistair took a moment to explain something I didn't know.

It was all quite bizarre. Was it one crime or three? What about the burnt-out cabin? Was that even connected? I asked Alistair, 'What do you think about the firebomb that happened a few weeks ago.'

Alistair looked surprised by the question. 'You are asking me if it is connected to Commander Yusef's death? Or what I think might have motivated it?'

'Either,' I replied. 'Something about how random it was sticks out. It appears to be without motivation, but tossing a petrol bomb into a person's cabin, in sure knowledge that it will kill them, is not a random act. It is one born of passion or anger. Strong emotions drive such things. Schneider suggested it might be connected to the saboteur – their first act.' Naming Schneider made the captain look at him and Schneider's cheeks flushed.

'Do you think that to be correct?' Alistair asked me.

I wasn't sure. 'The motivation could be the same. I just haven't worked out what that is yet.'

'It could be revenge,' suggested Jermaine, drawing attention his way. 'The person is damaging the ship and it has to be a crew member because of the places they have gone and the special knowledge they would need to be able to do what has been done. We know that already, but have you looked at watch patterns to narrow the pool of possible people? There might be a correlation between the times and who could have committed the crime each time.'

Schneider pulled a face. 'It was one of the first things we did,' he complained. 'We are not complete fools.'

Alistair held up a hand to stop him saying more. 'This is good. We are considering possibilities. Yes, we looked at that, but what about a former member of crew? What about someone who I fired, or who left after they were passed over for promotion? Could they have come back aboard as a passenger? Would they still be able to access the crew levels? When did we last change the access codes?'

Schneider's cheeks coloured. 'They are changed weekly, sir. Only the security team and bridge personnel are given the codes. The two-factor system: swipe card and code to input, has always been enough.'

'The code isn't fitted to every crew entrance though, is it? Some of the routes into the lower decks do not have the access code panel fitted so only a swipe card is required; those can be stolen, can't they, Patricia?' He chose to remind me that I liberated a master card from one of the cleaners when I was here previously.

Fighting the heat in my own cheeks, I cut my eyes at him playfully. 'We might be onto something with the former crew member. We are talking about two different things though. Is the saboteur the same person who killed Commander Yusef? Do any of us believe that?'

Lieutenant Schneider frowned. 'We shouldn't rule it out, Mrs Fisher.'

'No, we should not.' I agreed with him. I voiced my false opinion to see how those within earshot would react.

Baker appeared. 'We're going to move Commander Yusef to the morgue, sir,' he told Alistair. 'The available crew are lining the route down to the elevator. No one told them to, they just started doing it.'

Alistair started walking. 'Thank you for alerting me. I will help to carry the gurney.' And that was what he did, replacing one of the stewards to carry his second in command and friend down to the morgue where he would be held until the ship made port.

The superstructure was silent as the deputy captain passed through the passageways. Hats were doffed as his draped form was carried between the crew lining both walls. It was a sombre moment, but not inside my head where clues, factors, and considerations were colliding with each other in a maelstrom of confusion. One criminal or three? That was the question.

The respectfully silent passageways were suddenly, and very rudely, interrupted by a phone ringing loudly. Yup, you've guessed it. It was mine.

Muttering apologies, and ducking away from the press of people now following on as the stretcher continued on its journey, I rooted around in my handbag to find it. I should have thought to switch it to silent, but I hadn't, and now it was making trill noises as if giggling an evil laugh while it evaded my hand. Finally grasping the wretched device, I intended to stab the reject call button to shut it up, but the name displayed was Barbie.

'Patty!' she gasped when I answered it. 'Molly is here!'

Molly Returns

Jermaine heard Barbie's voice so I didn't have to explain my desire to get back to my suite. However, the procession of crew following the stretcher barred our path to the elevators and there was no other way down unless we went outside and climbed down the side.

Since we had to wait, I quizzed Barbie, 'Is she okay?'

'I think so,' she replied. 'She's not hurt. She says she met some people and ended up in their cabin drinking Sambuca. I don't even know what that is, but it sounds disgusting, Anyway, she fell asleep, and they put a blanket over her. She didn't hear her phone and when she woke up it was dead. She's in the kitchen now getting a snack.'

I felt relieved. Enormously relieved. Molly was safe and that meant several things. To start with, it meant my paranoia about the Godmother targeting her was unwarranted. The Godmother wasn't here; her agents and assassins hadn't picked off their first victim. It also meant I was looking at two crimes not three and suddenly it didn't seem that far-fetched for the two to be connected. Did Jermaine get it right and this is about revenge? Following that line of thinking, revenge for this person included murdering Commander Yusef. Like it or not, I was going to have to delve into the deputy captain's past. If there was something there which acted as a catalyst for this, maybe I would find it.

Ahead of us, the body of the deputy captain was disappearing inside the elevator. To Barbie I said, 'We're on our way to you now. I'll see you in a few minutes.' As the phone went back into my handbag, Alistair handed off the stretcher to the steward who would see Commander Yusef the rest of the way.

I tapped Lieutenant Baker on the arm. 'My missing person returned to my suite a few moments ago. She is unharmed and had fallen asleep in someone's cabin. I am on my way there now.'

'Well, that's a relief,' he replied carefully, making no mention of the untold manhours the security team had put into finding her.

'You are going to ask me about the saboteur and Commander Yusef, aren't you?' I asked but didn't bother to wait for his answer. 'I need a little time to think, plus some breakfast.' It wasn't yet five in the morning and the sun wouldn't be up for hours but my messed up body clock plus sleeping strange hours, and the snack-like meal I ate last night, meant I was too hungry to ignore the need for food. 'Then, I'll get back to you. I want to approach the two cases separately until we find a good reason to link them. I'm sure you have case notes for the saboteur, let's start by reviewing them together. You can bring me up to speed.'

Baker shot his cuff to check his watch. 'Is 0600hrs convenient?'

'Don't you need to sleep?' I asked him, aware that he had been up all night.

'Daylight will keep me going, Mrs Fisher. Schneider and I will get some food and join you in your suite at six.'

With the plan concocted, we split to go in different directions. Baker had people in Commander Yusef's cabin to oversee, and we were heading straight down in the next available elevator, but I took a few moments to let Alistair know Molly had returned.

He expressed his relief but had to return to the bridge. There was much to do, and he expected Commander Ochi soon.

At my suite, we found the door ajar. Surprised, but assuming someone was just the other side and about to close it, or perhaps just about to go out, Jermaine cautiously pushed it open.

I expected to find Barbie wearing her Lycra and about to go for a run. She'd been dead tired earlier, but her sleep got disturbed and this was her usual time to get up. She wasn't there though. No one was and the dogs didn't come out to greet me as they always would.

A sinking feeling filled my stomach as I made my way into the suite. Jermaine too, was worried, darting to look through Molly's open bedroom door.

I called out loudly, 'Anna!'

The response was instant, the barking of both my dogs coming from behind Barbie's bedroom door. It was closed, until Jermaine opened it. Anna and Georgie dashed out, their tails wagging madly in their excitement at seeing me and Jermaine.

From her bedroom, came groaning noises, followed a few seconds later by Barbie staggering out to see who was there. 'I took the girls to bed,' she told us. 'Molly said Anna tried to bite her when she let herself back in. Isn't that right, Molly?' she asked, swivelling to look at the kitchen. Clearly, she expected to see the younger woman still there. 'Did she go to bed? She said she wasn't tired.'

Molly probably wasn't tired. She'd had more sleep than the rest of us added together. However, she wasn't in her room. Jermaine confirmed that, going inside to make sure she wasn't using the bedroom's en suite bathroom.

'Her bag is on the bed,' he told us, holding it aloft for us to see. 'Her room key and phone are both in it.'

'Molly?' I called out, again raising my voice to a volume she couldn't possibly fail to hear. We all waited but no response came.

Barbie's forehead knitted into a frown. 'She was here ten minutes ago. I left her making a sandwich. I rescued her from the terror hounds and shut them in my room, made sure she was all right, and went back to bed. She was getting bread and things from the refrigerator.'

Jermaine went to look. 'There is a dirty plate and cup in the sink. It looks like she made herself a sandwich and ate it with some potato chips.'

She'd had time to eat and place the items neatly in the sink. 'Could she have gone back to see her new friends?' I asked. 'Did she tell you anything about them?'

Barbie was starting to look worried, her face reflecting the concern I now felt. We had her back but now she was gone again, and this time it looked more like she was taken. 'She said they were American, but that's all I know. They found her accent entertaining, or cute, I think she said, but I don't even know how many there were, or what age, or even if she made the whole thing up because she was hooking up with a guy.'

I was utterly in the dark again.

'Madam, you need to eat,' Jermaine pointed out. 'For cognitive function,' he added before I could argue. 'Molly may have realised she was missing an item and returned to her friends' cabin to collect it.'

My stomach grumbled hungrily at the thought. He was right about my needing to eat, and that Molly might be about to walk through the door again. Though, of course, we had her door card so she would have to knock. However, the point was I couldn't run off to save her because I didn't know where she was or if she even needed saving.

Accepting the need to fuel my body, I moved to the kitchen, but on my way, I voiced the thought now dominating my brain, 'Where are you, Molly?'

Captive

'Goodness, that is a lot of profanity from one small woman. Wherever did you learn such language?'

Molly spat back one of her favourite replies. It was advice on what he should do with himself and involved a monkey, a rhinoceros, a piece of yellow fruit, and an improbable act that involved him and the previous three things. She was twisting her head left and right and trying to see the man who was talking to her. She didn't like his accent. Not that she knew where it was from. It wasn't English and it wasn't American, but it sounded like English was his first language.

One of the men who had grabbed her wheezed and gasped still from the kick she swung between his legs. They knocked her out with something they had clamped over her face. She never even heard them coming. One moment she was putting her dirty plate and cup in the sink – best not to annoy Jermaine, he could be quite testy about cleanliness – the next she was being grabbed from behind. One of them grabbed her boobs as he put his arm around her chest, and she didn't think it was accidental; hence the kick in his spuds when she came around.

The voice behind her, remained behind her and she was tied to a chair now because of how she had struggled and fought. Around her chest was a man's belt. It was lashed so tight it was making it difficult to breathe. 'Can you loosen this a bit?' she begged.

'No,' replied the man she couldn't see. 'I can shoot you in the head though. Will that convince you to behave?'

She opened her mouth to make a snarky retort, thinking she should call his bluff because she didn't believe he was going to shoot her, but she heard him chamber a round, the distinct sound of a handgun's mechanism one she recognised from television and film. It stopped her from talking instantly. Especially when he placed the muzzle to the back of her head.

'What is your relationship with Patricia Fisher?' he asked.

Confused by the question, because she thought he was asking if she was in a relationship with her, she asked, 'What?'

'Your relationship,' he repeated. 'Daughter, niece, ward? I want to know how deeply I am cutting her when I kill you.'

He planned to kill her? All the moisture left her mouth and she felt sick. No, she was sick. The shock of his announcement overwhelmed her, the recently eaten sandwich making its way back to the light and onto the steel floor between her feet. Then she fainted.

With a sigh, the man calling himself Edward Smith placed the gun down. His two incompetents failed to take her handbag in which she would have her identification and the answer to the question about who she was to Patricia Fisher. He could send them back for it, but the chance of getting caught was too great. He had no idea the idiots would attempt to snatch her from the suite. He expected them to wait for the girl to venture out and snatch her in the dark. She was bound to be out when the bars were open, they could act as if she were drunk and they were escorting her safely back to her suite. One was wearing the uniform of a security officer after all. The two morons said it hadn't occurred to them.

He was going to kill her, just not yet. He had a masterful use for her that guaranteed not only would Patricia Fisher be too busy to interfere, but so too would the rest of the crew. Killing Commander Yusef had already yielded an unexpected bonus; Commander Ochi was to be the new deputy captain. Ochi, as a skilled engineer and head of the ship's engineering team, might have been able to work out what the man who called himself Edward Smith was up to. There were clues in his acts of sabotage if one looked at them holistically, but with Ochi suddenly thrust into a new role, his eyes would be too distracted to focus on the error reports being recorded from the ship's different systems.

It was all or nothing now. Soon, they would be looking for the girl. He didn't need to know who she was - his fantasy about listening to Patricia Fisher's voice while the girl cried tearfully down the phone to her, would have to remain just that – a fantasy. Even if they were not mother and daughter, there had to be a bond or why else would the older woman have the younger one along? Shortly, he would move her into position and set the final phase into motion.

They would never see it coming, and they would have no idea how to stop it.

Breakfast Session

Jermaine performed his usual kitchen miracles, presenting a sumptuous banquet for breakfast. As I tucked into my smoked salmon and poached eggs on warm sourdough toast with griddled, bacon-wrapped asparagus, I thought some more about what might motivate a person to damage the ship. None of the damage was lasting. If we all ignored the torched cabin, which could be fixed in time, all the measures the saboteur took were fixed within hours or days. The impact was on the passengers more than anyone else, their vacations affected negatively. Why though? Did I focus on that? Or on Commander Yusef's murder? My gut feeling was that they were not connected. Someone, a member of the crew, I felt certain, got into his cabin, and stabbed him in the chest. Sabotage and murder – were they connected. And where was Molly? There was no sign that she had been taken forcefully, and our frantic searching for her overnight had proven pointless because she returned of her own volition. However, she then vanished again.

One crime or three, the question echoed in my head. Further muddying the water was the missing captain's uniform. Was that just a random red herring and it wasn't missing at all? Commander Yusef's hat and shoes were taken though. Together with the clothing items taken from the dry cleaners, the thief had a complete outfit – a captain's uniform. But only if the thief and the killer were the same person. Or did someone steal Commanders Yusef's shoes and hat in a separate incident to his murder that was only brought to light by his death? The dots would not connect, and it felt like my head was spinning

A knock at the door interrupted my thoughts, making me realise the latest forkful of food had been halfway to my mouth for more than a minute. I looked across the suite to see Jermaine announcing Lieutenants Baker, Bhukari, Schneider, and Pippin. The hour's grace since I last saw them on the bridge had allowed me to get a shower and freshen myself. I was dressed, my breakfast was almost eaten, and I felt ready for the day. Now I had to hope they had something useful for me.

Just as the door was closing, a hand snuck through it, surprising Jermaine. It wasn't an intruder though, and it wasn't Molly returning, it was Sam Chalk responding to a text I sent him an hour ago. He ought to be asleep still, but I knew jet lag would have woken him early if the excitement of being somewhere new didn't. Either way, he was here, and introductions were required. 'Everyone, I would like you to meet, Sam Chalk. Sam is my assistant back home in England and quite the detective.'

'I have a magnifying glass,' he announced gleefully, pulling it from his jacket pocket. He met Baker, Schneider, Pippin, and Bhukari as they set out paperwork and two laptops on the breakfast bar.

With that task complete, I moved swiftly on to the next one. 'Listen, chaps, my missing housemaid, Molly. Well, she's still missing.' I got four sets of surprised eyebrows. 'Actually, it might be more accurate to say she is missing again.'

'I thought she came back by herself?' Schneider sought to clarify.

'She did,' said Barbie, joining the party from her room. 'I woke up when the dogs started barking. Molly was here long enough to make a sandwich but there is no sign of her now and this time she left her handbag, door card, and phone behind.'

I apologised. 'Sorry, team. I think we are back to having three problems to solve. Can we maybe find the people she was with last night?'

Barbie chipped in, 'She said they were American. I think we can assume they were around her age, but there's a danger she was lying because she was with a boy and didn't want to admit it.'

Baker and the others exchanged a glance. 'Put her picture on the community screens?' suggested Deepa.

Baker liked that idea. 'We can use the picture from yesterday, unless you have a better one?' he asked us.

Barbie slid in front of the computer that came as a furnishing of the suite. 'I'll go through her social media and see what I can find.' They were proposing to display a picture of our missing Molly on all the screens around the ship. There were hundreds of them. More normally they displayed information about what time the ship was due to dock, what onboard entertainment was happening where, or the top ten things to do where the ship was next due to dock. I had seen them display pictures of passengers before though – birthdays, milestone anniversaries, and other events typically. Her face, with an appeal to come forward if you met her yesterday, might get the result we wanted swiftly.

Pippin volunteered. 'I can arrange that. I just need the picture you want to use.' A smile crossed my face when I saw why he volunteered: he detached from the gaggle in uniform to go to Barbie where he stood just a little closer than was strictly necessary. I'd forgotten about his infatuation.

The Molly situation dealt with, so far as we could, it was time to look at what the security team had amassed on the saboteur. Then a memory surfaced. 'What was in the compartment under Commander Yusef's desk?'

My question caught Lieutenant Baker by surprise, but he blinked and replied, 'It was empty. Nothing in there but dust. No prints on the panel either. It's possible it was dislodged this evening, or it might have been like that for weeks, months, or years.'

'What have I missed?' The new voice cut through our conversation as Agent Garrett peered, blearily from the door of his room. That he had missed something was obvious; the room was full of people and activity at an hour which was earlier than decent. The combined jetlag, lack of sleep, plus frantic activity yesterday combined to let him sleep through the ruckus of Molly returning, dogs barking, and people coming in and out during the night.

'Molly is still missing,' I told him.

'There has been a murder,' said Jermaine, providing my bodyguard with another pertinent piece of information. I don't want to suggest that he didn't care about my missing housemaid, but it was Jermaine's announcement that got his attention.

'The Godmother's work?' he enquired, leaving his room to join the party at the breakfast bar. He was dressed already, freshly shaved and looking like a cop in an inexpensive suit, shirt, and tie. He carried his jacket in deference to the warmth in the room, hooking it over the back of a barstool as he looked for coffee.

'May I prepare you some breakfast,' asked Jermaine, the tone of his voice containing a hint of predatory growl. They were flirting again. The question about breakfast got the attention of everyone in the room except me. It seemed I was the only one who had eaten.

Soon, my butler was making breakfast for six people which suited me as we needed to spend the morning sifting evidence, mapping out events and looking for correlations. Jackets were removed and shoes kicked off as the team settled in and made themselves comfortable.

'What do we look at first, Mrs Fisher?' asked Sam.

The security team acted as if I were in charge and Sam's default setting as my assistant was to ask me questions and prompt my brain to work things out. 'I want to view this as two different cases. There is a saboteur, but until we find a reason to link the acts of sabotage to Commander Yusef's murder, we should treat it as a separate event.'

'What about Molly?' asked Barbie.

'I think she is being held by someone against her will, but whatever beef the saboteur has with the ship or the cruise line, I can't find a way to link that to me or her. It feels unconnected.' I sucked at my teeth for a second. 'Honestly, I hope she's with a boy and ran back to him after her sandwich this morning.'

Barbie pulled a face. 'That would be really irresponsible. She knew we were up half the night looking for her. I made sure she understood the problems her absence caused.'

'She's nineteen,' I pointed out. 'That's a great age for being irresponsible. Truthfully, I wish she would wander back through the door wanting sleep and exhausted from a night of … amorous activities, but I think we genuinely have a missing person case to solve. She must be on the ship. We should all hope Pippin's television message gets a result.'

Martin Baker tried to move the investigation forward. 'Okay. We are putting Molly to one side for a few moments. That gives us a murder, which had to be performed by a member of the crew, and the sabotage which also looked likely to be perpetrated by someone from the crew. Do we split into two teams and tackle them simultaneously?'

There was no reason not to, so that was what we did. Over the course of the next ninety minutes, we pulled apart the data they had and reviewed it, making notes and cross-checking dates and times. Jermaine produced six sumptuous breakfasts and kept the coffee going. I confess to thinking a buck's fizz sounded like a good pick-me-up this morning, but I stuck with the caffeine rather than fall into drinking at breakfast.

Our studies were interrupted by a call on the radio – someone had responded to Pippin's television idea.

Creepy Steward

I elected to go to them, wanting the exercise for the dogs and for myself, but also believing this was the start of tracking down my errant housemaid. At least, I hoped she was errant.

Sam came with me, my assistant by my side where I wanted him. Anna and Georgie happily led the way, dragging me along behind them even though they didn't know where they were going. The call over the radio came from the twelfth deck bursary where a young couple had been taken after they identified themselves to a crew member at breakfast.

Walking just behind me, as always, was Agent Garrett. He was yet to discover that I had been out and about without him during the night. Lieutenant Schneider also came along at my request because this was an official enquiry for the ship's security team.

It didn't take long to get there, though I insisted we take the stairs on the way down for some exercise. The couple were Blake and Jackson Schroder from St Louis. They were introduced that way and since I didn't think either name was necessarily male or female, I didn't know which was which. Clearly though, Jackson was an abbreviation or contraction of Jack's son, so I looked expectantly at the woman and asked, 'Blake have you seen or heard from Molly this morning?'

Blake, it turned out, was the guy, which made Jackson a girl's name somehow. He answered without commenting on my faux pas. 'No, she left our cabin around five this morning. She looked so tired we let her sleep.'

'We were playing cards with another couple,' added Jackson. 'We met them on board just a few days ago. They're this really nice gay couple from Boston, Casey and Gunnar.' Blake and Jackson looked like clean living people; the kind you see doing magazine commercials because they look so wholesome. They were in their mid-twenties and had that vibrant youthful look that suggests eating well, going to church, and doing lots of exercise.

'How did you meet Molly?' I asked. I suspected talking to them would prove to be a dead end, but I was short of leads to follow.

'She was sitting next to us on her lounger,' explained Jackson. 'She seemed to be all by herself and Blake had gone to the bar, so I asked her if she was here with someone and we got talking. She has such a cute accent. I just wanted to listen to her talking. It was like having a conversation with *Mary Poppins*.'

'And you invited her back to your cabin?' I queried, thinking it a little forward and wondering how it came about.

Sensing that my question had a hint of impropriety about it, Blake began to bristle, but his wife answered, 'There was someone watching her.' My heart thudded in my chest and suddenly everyone in the bursary was paying attention to what the woman had to say next. Her face coloured when she realised everyone was hanging off her next words. 'It was a creepy-looking steward,' she told us.

'Creepy how?' asked Schneider.

'He was watching her,' said Blake. 'I wanted to confront him, but Jackson didn't want me to cause a scene, so we all left. That was when Casey and Gunnar suggested a game of cards.'

'What did you play?' asked Agent Garrett. It seemed like a silly question that would interrupt the flow of the interview, but I knew he was asking it to see how they reacted. If either struggled to provide an answer, or they looked at each other for confirmation first, or just plain looked like they were panicking, then it would reveal they were lying and that would throw doubt on everything they said.

However, Jackson's instantaneous response was, 'Rummy. We would have played bridge but that's not a game for five.' She was telling the truth.

I took over again. 'How sure are you that the steward was watching Molly and not someone else?'

She looked at her husband before answering. 'It was more that Molly said he was watching her.'

'She used the word 'perving' to describe it,' Blake explained. 'It's not a word I am familiar with, but we got what she meant. She claimed he kept looking at her bum.'

'Which was really cute,' giggled Jackson. 'Such a British thing to say.'

'Did he approach her?' I asked.

They both shook their heads. 'No. He was loitering near the pool bar. He had a tray but there were never any drinks on it and we never saw him serve anyone. He walked around like the other stewards, only where they were taking orders and serving drinks, he was pretending to so that he could look at Molly. At least, that's what she said.'

Schneider had a question, 'Molly Lawrie is staying in a suite. Do you know why she didn't return there when she left the pool?'

Jackson's cheeks coloured again. 'Um, she said she felt out of place. Are you her employer?' she asked me.

Okay, I got where she was coming from. At nineteen, I wouldn't have relished hanging out with a woman in her fifties. Pushing it to the side, I asked, 'Can you describe the steward?'

Jackson produced her phone. 'I can do better than that. I got his picture in case we needed to report him.'

Her announcement was like getting a jolt of electricity. It wasn't a home run, but it sure felt like we were moving forward all of a sudden. Especially when Schneider squinted at the tiny screen and said, 'I know that guy. That's Harry Tomlinson. I've had reason to speak with him before. He almost got fired a few months back.' His eyes rolled to the top of his head as he searched his memory. 'It was something to do with drugs. That's all I remember. He went before the deputy captain – the deputy captain deals with all crew discipline matters,' he explained. 'It wasn't a case I was involved in, but I remember it because Baker was, and he was livid when Tomlinson got off with a warning. The deputy captain said there wasn't enough evidence. There was a bit of a stink at the time because we all felt we had more than enough to eject him from the ship.' He nodded as the memory flooded back. 'Yeah. He was caught with marijuana in his cabin, but he said it wasn't his and he didn't know how it got there ...'

Schneider was still talking, but I was no longer listening. I was spit-balling ideas in my head and wondering if Tomlinson might have targeted Yusef because of something to do with the discipline hearing. Yusef let him off though, so that didn't make sense. I missed whatever Schneider said next, but didn't get him to repeat it, he was on his radio already, putting out a ship alert to the security team. Tomlinson was to be apprehended. He might be innocent of taking Molly, but something told me he was involved at some level in whatever the heck was going on.

What's the Worst They Could Have Planned?

I didn't accompany Schneider when he departed to find Harry Tomlinson. Tomlinson was a Steward third class, literally the bottom rung of ranks on the ship and he'd been stuck at that level for five years since he came on board. Schneider provided a look at his personnel record, where I quickly learned he was from just outside Nottingham, twenty-seven years old, and had a staff discipline record that made it surprising he was still employed.

Expecting they would swiftly locate and arrest him, I took Sam and the dogs, and returned to my suite where the team were still delving into the clues we had.

'We identified a man who was watching Molly,' said Sam as he came into the suite's main area.

Jermaine took the dog leads from my hand as I followed my young assistant. 'Thank you, sweetie.' Jermaine acknowledged my thanks with a prim nod as I swept into the central living area.

Baker held his radio aloft. 'We heard. Tomlinson has been skating on thin ice for a long time, but snatching a passenger would be a change of pace. Apart from the marijuana, he's never shown any criminal behaviour. He's mostly just lazy. What would motivate him to take her?'

I dreaded to think. Honestly, I hoped it was because he was dealing drugs again and my housemaid was looking to score some. I would have to let her go if that were the case, but it was still better than what the alternatives might be. Was he a sexual predator? I didn't wish to speculate. To answer Baker, I said, 'We should know soon enough. How have things progressed here?'

I got a few shrugs in response. 'We cannot narrow it down finely enough for our results to be of any use,' said Barbie. 'If we assume the acts of sabotage are being committed by someone who is off duty at the time, the events do not line up. Anyone who looks likely for one event, is working when the next two occur.'

Baker scratched his head. 'It's a false assumption too. They could easily be on duty when they commit the acts. If they are attacking the fire alarm system or the public address system, it might be better for them if they are supposed to be doing some maintenance. That way there is less chance of them being questioned.' It was a valid point.

Adding up what they were telling me, I concluded, 'We're nowhere then?'

Jermaine, who had been just as stuck into the research as everyone else said, 'That would appear to be the case, madam. We need a fresh angle of approach.'

'What about Commander Yusef?' I asked. Pippin had been looking at that with Baker. 'Anything back from the crime scene analysis?' I was being hopeful, but I knew how limited their resources were. They held only a fraction of the equipment of a police crime lab back home. They could check for prints, but they were using old techniques, and they could swab for hair and fibre, but didn't have the equipment to analyse DNA.

Baker left the emotion out when he reported, 'There were no prints on the murder weapon. Dr Kim confirmed the blade penetrated his heart, puncturing the left ventricle to guarantee death within a few minutes. He may have held on for a while because the knife was left in to seal the wound but there was no way he could have been saved. The blade is a generic kitchen knife, most likely taken from one of the onboard galleys where there are hundreds of them. They are not monitored or counted.

There were no pieces of flesh beneath his fingernails to suggest he fought his attacker, and we found no fingerprints other than his and a few from the cleaners who keep his quarters tidy. There was nothing to find,' he concluded. 'Someone with the bridge access code and a swipe card came up in the elevator last night, got into his cabin past another security door and killed him with a knife that they most likely took with them. Premeditated or otherwise, it's still murder.'

'What was Commander Yusef doing in his quarters? He was on duty, wasn't he?'

Baker understood why I asked the question. 'Yes, Mrs Fisher. However, he, the captain, and two other senior officers perform the role of watch commander. The watch commander is there to make decisions should any be necessary, but they will habitually busy themselves with other tasks. They are not required to remain on the bridge for the duration of their eight-hour watch.'

I hadn't known that. 'Then it wasn't random for him to return to his accommodation, and the killer, once inside, could wait until Commander Yusef entered. The victim would never see the attack coming.'

Jermaine had a different theory. 'It could have been someone who knocked on the door and stabbed Commander Yusef when he opened it. That way there is no need to circumvent the door security.'

The room fell silent. More than two hours of staring at dates, times, clues, and snippets of information and we hadn't achieved a thing. All we had was conjecture.

Lieutenant Schneider came to our aid. Sort of.

The crackle of radio as he tried to raise Lieutenant Baker was heard by us all.

'Baker, go,' Lieutenant Baker replied.

Schneider's Austrian accent cut over the airwaves. 'Word got out that we were looking for him and he scarpered before we could get to his duty station. He's supposed to be working the eighteenth deck cabin service today. He reported for duty but hasn't been seen since. We are on our way to his cabin on deck four now. Over.'

Baker held his radio to his mouth. 'Roger. Keep us informed.' When he let go of the send button, he looked about the room. 'Tomlinson is starting to look good for being involved in something.'

'But not for the sabotage, because he's a steward and wouldn't have the knowledge to do what has been done, and not for the murder of Commander Yusef because, again, he's a steward and wouldn't have the access code,' I pointed out. Frustrated, I went back to my original notes. 'There's something we've missed here. The saboteur must have a purpose to his actions. These aren't mindless acts of vandalism. If a person wanted to do that, they could set off fire extinguishers, set fires, break things, block the toilets. The things the saboteur has done require skill and planning. To me, that means they are motivated, and it suggests there is an end goal.'

'But what might that be?' asked Barbie, getting involved. 'Could it be Commander Yusef's murder?'

'Damage the ship's reputation?' suggested Pippin.

'Embarrass the captain?' hazarded Bhukari.

I shook my head. The back of my skull was itching, letting me know we were onto something. 'What would be the worst they could do?' I voiced my question aloud. 'What is the most devastating thing they could have planned?'

'Kill a load of passengers,' suggested Pippin.

Jermaine huffed out a worried sigh and said, 'Cripple the ship?'

His suggestion got a gasp from everyone and no one said anything in response. We all just looked at each other until Lieutenant Baker murmured, 'I think I'd better speak with the captain.'

Double Cross

Harry Tomlinson was struggling to contain his rising panic. Nicholai called to let him know the security team were looking for him. The warning allowed him to leave his place of work before they found him there, but where was he supposed to go? Nicholai said to head directly to the boss. The man they were calling Edward Smith had been on the ship for three weeks now without detection, but no one was looking for him, they would be looking for Harry and he knew it.

With nowhere else to go, and craving the comfort of having the boss tell him what to do, he ran whenever there was no one around to see him, and avoided as many people as possible as he made his way down to the bottom of the ship. Could he hide down there with the boss? They would make port in a few days and he would be able to sneak off with Nicholai's help. All Harry would have to do is time it so that Nicholai was one of the guards at the crew exit.

The small ray of hope that he might be able to evade capture died when he got to the boss's secret room.

'It's Nicholai,' the man calling himself Edward Smith wheezed from the floor. 'He wants all the money. He even wants your share. I couldn't stop him! I retrieved it last night as you know, but Nicholai has it now.'

Harry looked down at the man's shirt, soaked deep red with blood. He began to kneel, instinct making him try to give aid.

'Don't!' the man insisted, putting a weak arm out to stop Harry coming any closer. 'There's no point. I want you to save yourself. Nicholai took the ship's blueprints and a stack of other evidence. He's putting it in your cabin even as we speak.'

Harry's jaw dropped. 'Why!'

'To tie the sabotage to you. He even took the girl's bikini briefs. He'll plant them in your cabin and leave you to carry the can. He's already stolen all the money.'

'But I will just say it was him,' argued Harry, failing to see the bigger picture.

'He's on the security team. He'll corner you and shoot you, Harry,' wheezed the man, clutching his chest and trying to stay conscious. 'Take my gun. Get to him first. Maybe you can beat him to your cabin. He had his arms full of the evidence he plans to plant and would have to go slow to avoid other people. Get there first! Kill him and live your life, Harry.'

'What about the girl?' Harry gasped, unable to believe what was happening.

'Don't you hear me, man!' the man calling himself Edward Smith shouted, 'You can deal with the girl later. She's seen your face, but she's sealed in the container now and cannot escape. Now run, Harry! Run, and beat Nicholai at his own game. You can kill him and plant the evidence in his cabin. Take his door card and kill the girl with Nicholai's weapon. You can get away scot free, boy. But only if you hurry!'

The man who wanted them to call him Edward Smith thrust the handgun across the floor with the arm he was using to support his dying body. The weapon was bloody, but it would work.

Terrified beyond belief, Harry picked it up. The boss's suggested plan could work. Pin it on Nicholai instead: kill him then leave an evidence trail back to the boss and the dead body of the girl. He could make it look like Nicholai killed the girl and the boss, and the boss managed to kill Nicholai before his wounds finished him. The security team would still have questions for Harry, but maybe he would just get fired. That sounded like a great result from where he stood.

Cursing himself for trusting the Russian, Harry picked up the gun. 'Go!' the boss bellowed one last time and it put fire in Harry's belly. He had no choice now. All the cards were on the table. He either got Nicholai, or Nicholai got away with the money leaving Harry to go to jail for murder, arson, and more.

Suicide Note

In my suite, we listened intently to Lieutenant Schneider's report over the radio. He was in Steward Third Class Tomlinson's cabin on deck four where they found everything they could possibly want to find. According to Schneider, it was a treasure trove of evidence, the like of which he had never before seen.

'He's the saboteur,' he told us. 'And he killed Commander Yusef.'

'You can be certain of that?' asked Baker, his eyes pinched in disbelief and confusion. Like me, his feet were most likely twitching with a need to go to the scene and see it for himself.'

Schneider's voice contained no emotion at all when he replied with, 'It's all in his suicide note.'

'He's dead!' blurted Barbie. Sam's eyes went as wide as dinner plates.

I was sitting on a couch, fussing Anna and Georgie while drinking a cup of tea which Jermaine had recently served. I could sit no longer though.

Schneider said, 'He's not here, and the note on his computer doesn't say how he planned to kill himself. He might have gone overboard for all we know. He confesses to the sabotage and explains why – it's all to do with being passed over for promotion. That's why he killed Commander Yusef too though his suicide note claims Yusef was blackmailing him. I'm having trouble believing that part. Tomlinson's note goes on to explain how he got onto the bridge and stabbed the deputy captain when he opened his cabin door. Not only that, there's a framed picture of Commander Yusef and his family. It was taken in front of the castle at Disney World in Florida. I remember Commander Yusef telling me about the holiday and I remember where I last saw the picture: it was on the desk in his cabin.'

Standing up I said, 'We have to go. We need to see what he is seeing.' Nobody disagreed, not even Agent Garrett who would be content to lock me in my suite for however long we were going to be on board. It was impossible, with all that was going on, to hide that I had been out of the cabin during the night. He was unhappy about it, but there really wasn't anything he could do to stop me moving freely unless he watched my every move and slept blocking my bedroom door. I was playing along the best that I could, but I wasn't convinced there was any danger to me currently.

Unplugging my phone from its charger and gathering my things to put them in my handbag, it became clear that everyone was coming. Barbie had dashed to her room to get her running shoes – they went so well with her skin-tight Lycra, and the three security team were all shuffling back into their jackets and hats, vying for space in front of the mirror by the suite's main entrance as they all needed to look their best for going out in public. Besides, the captain was bound to take a personal interest and he wouldn't abide scruffiness.

Baker was on his radio even as we went out of the door.

'Stay close, please, Mrs Fisher,' insisted Agent Garrett, his polite request really nothing of the sort. I didn't reply.

The radio chatter was fast; back and forth between multiple users on the security band as they coordinated the search for Steward Tomlinson. Every member of the team, on watch or not, had been roused on the captain's orders and more crew members recruited to help with the search. Finding the saboteur before he could kill himself, or if he were dead, before a passenger found his body, was instantly bumped to the top of the list of things to do.

Would he commit suicide publicly? That was the question. He could just slip over the side of the ship and into the icy water. No one would ever know if he did. He might have already done so, but he could equally pick somewhere public to end his life, like diving off the balcony on deck nineteen. It plunges four decks through the centre of the ship to bring light and air where the largest congregation of shops and restaurants can be found.

We were heading down to join Schneider in Tomlinson's cabin, but we weren't all going to get there. The voice of someone I didn't recognise cut through the airwaves, doing their best to coordinate the security detail and other crew involved in the onboard manhunt.

'Is that Commander Ochi?' I asked Deepa, targeting her with my question simply because she was next to me in the passageway. Our shoulders were bumping together as we hurried onward.

'Yes,' she nodded. 'He's having a heck of a first day as the new deputy captain.' I already knew the deputy captain was also the head of ship's security and wondered what background and experience Commander Ochi had if he was now in charge.

He wanted Baker to meet him on deck eighteen and he was to bring whoever he had with him. He meant crew of course, not me and my friends or Agent Garrett.

'Good luck, guys,' gasped Barbie, waving the security team members goodbye as they jogged in one direction and we went the other.

Coming into the wide area that housed the nearest elevators and the start of the ship's central shopping and recreation area, there were bewildered passengers whispering to each other and pointing as they saw another member of crew rush by. One, a woman with a map of the ship in her hands, tried to ask a question of a steward. He dismissed her rudely - which was not the right thing to do - and left her looking disgruntled.

'That wasn't very nice,' murmured Sam.

'They really have everyone involved,' agreed Barbie.

'Tomlinson's been sabotaging the ship,' Wayne pointed out. 'He created mass panic yesterday. And we now know he murdered the deputy captain. If he hasn't yet committed suicide, what might he have yet planned as his final act? They need to stop him, and they need to do it fast.'

'They need to capture him,' I added. 'They need him alive if he is the one who took Molly. I want to know where she is.'

There was no need to reply, and no one did. We all hurried onward, into the elevator, and down to deck seven where we had to exit and look for a crew elevator that would get us down to deck four.

My feet moved themselves, my brain wasn't required for the task, which was a good thing because it was engaged in trying to guess what might have triggered Tomlinson. He'd been on this ship for five years, stuck in the same rank with no sign of advancement. In fact, according to Schneider, he was lucky to still have a job and had the deputy captain to thank for that. I didn't believe Tomlinson's claim that Yusef was blackmailing him. Or ... I didn't want to believe it. It didn't fit with my mental image of the former deputy captain, but I had to accept I could be wrong.

The doors of the crew elevator swished open, giving us access to deck four where most of the crew were accommodated. I was here only a few hours ago with Baker and Schneider. Admittedly, it was yesterday, but I was yet to clock up twenty-four hours on board and had managed to cram a lot into my cruise already – none of it was what I'd hoped for or intended.

'Which way?' asked Sam, peering cautiously left and right along the narrow passageway. I too was waiting for either Barbie or Jermaine to lead. The crew accommodation was a rabbit warren of passageways, navigable only by the indoctrinated, or by making sure one accessed it using an elevator that would deliver you close to the place you wanted to go.

Barbie set off, skipping ahead to check the number on the wall of the cross section to our right. 'It should be this way,' she advised, but just as she turned the corner, a door opposite us opened and the figure coming through it froze.

Staring right at me was Steward Third Class Harry Tomlinson and he had a gun in his hand.

Need Him Alive!

His eyes flared in panic. I couldn't tell if he recognised me, but he knew we had seen his gun, our eyes all locking on it before flicking up to his face.

My lips parted as I started to speak, I wanted to shout a warning to Sam, but the words never got a chance to reach the air because Agent Garrett slammed me into the bulkhead. Throwing his body in front of mine, Wayne's right hand was pulling his gun from the holster beneath his left arm.

Tomlinson saw the movement, interpreted it correctly, and raised his own gun.

Barbie squealed and ducked. She was closest to him but in the mouth of a cross passage she was able to use for cover.

Tomlinson's gun fired, the shot barely aimed as he turned and ran back through the door. I felt it though. I felt it because it slammed into Agent Garrett, shunting him backward and into me, knocking me off balance so I lost my footing. My hands scrambled for purchase to keep me upright, snagged Wayne's jacket, and pulled him with me as I fell. He landed on top of me, forcing the air from my lungs but there was only one message flashing in my brain: He'd thrown himself in front of a bullet for me!

Barbie screamed, the ear-splitting sound one of shocked reaction to the booming noise of the gun going off.

I was partially trapped beneath Wayne, his bodyweight pinning my legs to the deck. I had to check his condition! He'd been shot, the bullet striking him somewhere on his upper torso, so I was frantically trying to get out from under him, but also trying to be gentle with him as I dragged myself free.

'Oh, my God! Oh, my God, Wayne!' I stuttered, trying to get around so I could stem the bleeding or create a tourniquet – whatever was needed.

Sam was there already, trying to help our wounded man. 'I'm fine,' Wayne winced, sounding nothing of the sort. He tried to sit up but grunted in pain. 'I'm fine. My vest stopped it,' he managed to add with another wince. Then he thrust his weapon along the deck to Jermaine's feet. 'Take it!' he snarled. 'Get him!'

We could all hear Tomlinson running away, his footsteps echoing back toward us from behind the closed door. He didn't fire any more shots, but before Jermaine could pick up Wayne's gun, if that were what he planned to do, the sound of boots on the steel floor erupted from the side passageway Barbie had ducked down.

I heard her shouting excitedly to someone, 'He went this way!'

Two seconds later, Schneider appeared, and he wasn't alone. The contingent of security guards from Tomlinson's cabin must have heard the shot and Barbie's scream. Their guns were drawn, and their faces meant business.

Barbie was pointing the way, standing back so the guards could chase their man. 'He's armed!' she told them. 'And he only fired one shot so far.'

Agent Garrett pushed himself to a seated position. He was hurt but he was okay, and I chose to leave him in favour of chasing Tomlinson.

Jermaine saw my intention. 'Sam and I will stay with him, madam,' he volunteered, dropping to one knee to check the policeman was truly unharmed.

Barbie's eyes were as wide as saucers. 'You're not going after them are you, Patty?' she squeaked. 'There's going to be shooting!'

'Where's Molly!' I shouted back as I raced past her. There were five, or maybe six of the security team ahead of me - I didn't count them as they ran by. They would protect me if it came to it, but since Molly clearly wasn't in Tomlinson's cabin, he must have stashed her, or her body, I mentally cringed, somewhere else. I needed to know where that was.

Barbie twitched with a moment of indecision, until Jermaine shouted, 'Go!' then she sprinted after me, catching and passing me in a matter of seconds with her gazelle-like speed.

Racing down the passageway, we passed more cross sections where Tomlinson could conceivably have gone, but Schneider was on his radio and coordinating everyone else. A woman's voice echoed in the tinny way voices sound over the radio. 'We've just spotted him! He's in K stairwell, heading up!'

We were close to his cabin when we saw him, and it looked like he was heading back to it. Why was he heading back to his cabin? That was the question dominating my thoughts. He'd written a suicide note for someone to find. Maybe he knew they would catch him. Maybe it was always his plan to kill himself. Whichever it was, it looked to me that he'd had a change of heart or couldn't bring himself to go through with it. He had a gun: all he had to do was pull the trigger.

The voices bouncing back and forth over the radio were getting more and more excited. It sounded like they had him cornered and he was going to surrender. In my head, I breathed a sigh of relief.

That was when I heard the shot.

It came over the radio, but we also heard it echoing in the passageway just as we got to the stairwell. I could barely dare to breathe as the team ahead of me pushed through the doors and onto a landing. They were making their way up, but Commander Ochi's voice came over the radio again, cutting over the chatter when he demanded, 'Report!'

On the landing above us, we could hear an argument, what sounded like a heated discussion about whether Tomlinson had been surrendering or not.

'He was lifting his gun!' a man insisted.

'He twitched!' a woman shouted back at him. 'He was going to put it down!'

'He was going to shoot you!' the first voice argued.

Over the radio came Commander Ochi's voice again, 'Report!' he shouted, sounding angry at being made to wait.

The female officer replied to his demand, 'Tomlinson's dead, sir.'

Unhappy Hero

Commander Ochi arrived just a few moments after we did. We came up the stairs to deck five and he came down from deck seven where they accessed the stairwell right at the top. It was a blank steel stairwell, never intended to be seen by passengers and it echoed loudly each time anyone moved or spoke.

Steward Third Class Harry Tomlinson was covered by a jacket so people didn't have to see his eyes staring pointlessly to heaven. He was shot at close range by a member of the security team, the bullet passing through his neck to seal his fate in an instant.

Commander Ochi, now head of ship's security – one of many roles the deputy captain fulfils - was swift to shake the hand of the man responsible for the deadly shot, an unseemly thing to do standing so close to the poor man's body. 'Your name?' he enquired of the bewildered looking man.

'Lieutenant Mashkov, sir. Lieutenant Nicholai Mashkov.'

Commander Ochi pumped the man's arm, unaware how crass it looked to do so. Lieutenant Mashkov looked embarrassed and a bit sick. There was no further mention or debate about whether Tomlinson was going to fire his weapon or not. The female officer we found with the body had stopped insisting Tomlinson was trying to surrender. Undoubtedly, she understood it could be argued, but never proven, and to accuse Lieutenant Mashkov again now would shroud her as a troublemaker among her fellow officers.

'I want a full debrief and report from everyone here by end of watch,' Commander Ochi ordered. 'Remove this garbage to the morgue,' he growled, 'and show me his cabin. Who was leading the inspection there?'

'That would be me, sir,' volunteered Schneider.

He got a nod from the Commander. 'Very good. Lead on.'

'Wait.' My voice stopped everyone dead in their tracks. 'Molly Lawrie is still missing. Her bikini briefs were found in his cabin, correct?' I asked Schneider to confirm.

He nodded. 'That's right, sir. It looks like Tomlinson grabbed the missing passenger as well as murdering Commander Yusef. It also looks like he committed all the acts of sabotage.'

The deputy captain pursed his lips. 'Then we must hurry. Tomlinson cannot tell us where she is but there may be clues in his cabin.'

'Or on his person,' I pointed out, sad that I was better at this than the professional security surrounding me.

Darting forward, Lieutenant Mashkov dealt with the task, removing the jacket draped over the body to reveal the mess the bullet made. I looked away, unwilling to let my eyes linger.

'There's nothing,' Mashkov declared a few moments later. 'Just his wallet. His cabin door card is in that, but there's nothing else in his pockets.'

Commander Ochi started down the stairs. 'To his cabin then.'

Leaving Mashkov and all the others behind, Schneider led his original team back down the steel staircase. Right at the front, next to Schneider, was Commander Ochi. I couldn't recall ever seeing him before. Of course, there was a lot of crew on this ship and he ran the engineering division so was most likely engaged in activities away from the passenger area most of the time. He was in his late fifties, grey dominating his jet-black hair which was cut short in the style expected of male crew members. At five feet eight inches, he was short by comparison with most of the men around him, and he carried a little paunch around his waist – Looking at his back as I followed him down the stairs, I could see bulging love handles. I didn't know anything about him, but I expected he would be no better or worse than any of the other deputy captains I'd met.

Thinking that reminded me just how many second in commands there had been since I came on board. Before Yusef was a woman called Shriver. She left when it became untenable for her to remain in her post. Before her was another Japanese man. His name was Ikari. He and I got on well, as opposed to Shriver who butted heads with me constantly. Ikari left when an axe, thrown by a maniac intent on killing me, ended his career prematurely. He survived but would never go to sea again. He said he was glad for it, and happily retired to be at home with his family. My face chose to frown all by itself when I thought about who Ikari replaced and the back of my skull itched.

Why would my skull itch at the memory of Robert Schooner?

The party turned a corner where we found Jermaine, Sam, and Agent Garrett.

'Are you all right, Mrs Fisher?' asked Sam.

I patted his arm to thank him for being concerned as I made my way to check on Agent Garrett. 'I'm fine, Sam. Just worried about Molly.'

The policeman was back on his feet and had his shirt stripped open. On the deck was his jacket and the bulletproof vest he'd worn. The Kevlar might have stopped the bullet, but he had a terrible bruise where the bullet struck. His skin was already discoloured and threatened to turn black all around the bright red pock mark to the right of his left nipple. Tomlinson might not have aimed his shot, but he still hit Wayne's heart. Jermaine bent to pick the vest off the deck and held it up for me to see when I approached.

'Are you sure you're all right, Wayne?' I asked him. I'd been mostly cool towards my appointed bodyguard, not really wanting him along and probably making him feel that way. Now, given that he'd stopped a bullet which might have killed me and gave not one thought to his own mortality, I didn't see how I could be anything other than grateful.

'I am sore,' he admitted.

'You saved me,' I said meekly, knowing I was not deserving of the sacrifice he almost made. What if the bullet had hit his head?

All he said in reply was, 'I have orders.'

'That was quite the shot.' observed Schneider. 'The vest did its job.'

Wayne nodded, taking the bulletproof garment from my butler's hand to inspect it. 'Only just,' he said, pointing out where the bullet had gone all the way through the fabric, only to stop as the nose of the round protruded the other side.'

'I think he has at least one broken rib,' claimed Jermaine. Wayne cut his eyes at the tall Jamaican – he didn't want us to know he was injured.

'I'll be fine,' he insisted. To prove the point, he started buttoning up his shirt again, but I could see he was gritting his teeth against the discomfort he felt.

He wanted to carry on, and I didn't think he was going to fall down dead, but I wasn't happy for him to continue his duties until he'd been checked out. What if the bullet had chipped a piece of rib away from the bone which was now floating about inside his chest? I didn't know if that was possible, but as I thought about what might be best for him, he chose to use the bulkhead for support and demonstrated how hurt he was.

'Jermaine, please help Agent Garrett to find sickbay,' I requested, and held up a finger to stop Wayne protesting. 'I am surrounded by armed men and women, Agent Garrett. I will find you in sickbay shortly, or back at my suite if the doctor gives you the all clear.'

Wayne didn't look happy about it but nodded and accepted a helping hand from Jermaine. Schneider, Ochi, and most of the security team had already pushed on, keen to get to Tomlinson's cabin, and with Wayne now heading for medical treatment, Molly was back as my immediate priority. 'We should push on,' I said to Barbie and Sam. 'Molly is still missing.'

Tomlinson's cabin was just around the corner, less than a hundred yards from where we met him. It was also easy to spot which door was his because it was open, surrounded by the security team, and the belongings inside were being laid out all over the deck outside.

'It's going to take us a while to catalogue it all,' said Lieutenant Schneider.

I had been wondering how his team of six all managed to fit and operate inside Tomlinson's tiny cabin. The answer was that they didn't. Two were working inside, the other four were in the passageway, laying Tomlinson's items out on the deck and grouping them. It was curiously efficient as it meant they could completely empty his cabin, grouping personal items in one place, and putting evidence in another. The evidence, such as the framed photograph of Commander Yusef and his family were in clear plastic bags.

'Is there any need for this now?' asked Commander Ochi. 'Sentence has been passed, one might say,' he made a little joke that no one laughed at. Seeing that his humour was off the mark, he quickly doused the smile on his face and with a more serious expression asked, 'We can see he did it. You say you have a written confession. Is there any need for a painstaking gathering of evidence?'

Lieutenant Schneider eyed his superior carefully, assessing whether the man was serious or not before saying, 'We need to satisfy ourselves that he was guilty. We also need to determine why he committed his crimes and be assured that he was working alone.'

Ochi's face showed surprise. 'You think he might have an accomplice?' The concept clearly hadn't occurred to the Commander if his tone was anything to go by.

'We need to rule it out,' Schneider replied.

'Is there anything to suggest where he might have taken Molly?' I enquired hopefully. 'A set of keys? A mark on one of the schematics? Anything that might provide a clue to where she is. Dead or alive, I need to find her.' I didn't want that sweet, innocent girl to be dead, but the longer she was missing, the more likely it would be.

One of the female officers held up a clear plastic evidence bag. In it was a pair of yellow string bikini bottoms that I last saw cutting Molly's backside in two. A ball of worry formed in my stomach.

'That's all we have to tie him to her disappearance,' said Schneider. 'It's damning evidence though because I don't see how he could get them if he weren't the one who took her.'

'I think those are hers,' said Barbie, her voice barely more than a whisper. She was biting her lip and looking scared for our young friend. 'If only Mashkov hadn't shot Tomlinson. He could have told us where she was.'

Schneider looked down at me. 'We'll keep going, Mrs Fisher.' His voice was as quiet as Barbie's, a reverent hush as if we were all talking about Molly in the past tense. 'One way or another, we'll find her.'

Looking back up at him, I said, 'I need to think. I feel like there is something missing here. He had a gun, yet he used a knife to kill Commander Yusef.'

Schneider thought about that. 'He was on the bridge, Mrs Fisher. If he used the gun, he would have been heard.'

'But we met him on his way back to his cabin. He was heading there, and he was still alive. If he wrote a suicide note, then why didn't he kill himself in his cabin with the gun he had. Why go somewhere else?'

Schneider shrugged. 'We'll never know.'

I had no further argument to raise, no more points to make. There was something wrong with what I was seeing, I just didn't know what it was.

Picking it Apart

'What is it that bothers you, Patty?' Barbie and I were sitting on the couches in my suite with the dogs. I had Anna tucked onto my lap where she had curled up like a cat. Georgie was spread out on her back along Barbie's legs and looked to have been shot or maybe dropped from a great height. Jermaine had left Agent Garrett with Dr Davis in the sickbay and was serving tea with petit fours at my request.

'Tomlinson has been on this ship for five years and suddenly decides to sabotage it, murder the deputy captain, and kidnap a passenger. He also murdered Edgar Thomas, I would assume.' I was running it all through my head, trying to make it fit when I was sure it didn't. There was something wrong about the whole thing. 'Could he do all the things he did alone? Could he patch his way into the address system? If we assume one man can do that, did Tomlinson have the technical ability? He was a steward, the lowest rank in the most menial job. How would he know how to shut off the bilge pumps or access the ship's fire warning system command wire?'

'He snapped?' suggested Sam. 'He could have picked up how to do things along the way. He's been on the ship for five years.'

I pursed my lips. It didn't feel right. 'What about the cabin he firebombed?'

'We don't know that the firebombing is connected, Patty,' Barbie reminded me. I was the only one thinking my line of thought. Everyone else was content the criminal onboard had been caught and killed. Why couldn't I let it go?

'Whose cabin was firebombed?' asked Sam, reminding me that he wasn't with us at that point.

I opened my mouth to tell him, but the name wouldn't come. I glanced across to Jermaine, hoping he would remember.

I got a frown in return. 'It was a lady from Botswana. A chef,' he supplied, which was about as much as I could remember. Then he said, 'It was next door to your old cabin, Barbie.'

'Really?' she asked, sounding surprised. 'Left or right?'

'Hold on,' I interrupted. 'You used to live opposite each other?'

Barbie turned her face to look at me. 'Yes, that's how we met. Well, actually we met when we came on board the ship because we started on the same day and had to do all our induction and orientation together. But we might not have seen each other after that if we hadn't been directly across the passageway from each other.'

The back of my skull was itching like mad now.

'Who was in that cabin before the chef from Botswana?' I demanded to know.

Again, Barbie asked, 'Was it the cabin to my left or the one to the right as you look at it?'

'To the right.' Jermaine's reply hit me like an uppercut.

I must have gasped or choked or something. I felt like I was having an out of body experience because I couldn't hear anything anyone was saying. My vision threatened to spin as I fought to get oxygen to my brain.

There were hands on me, people grabbing my arms.

Sam's face was a worried mask and Barbie was in my face. 'Patty! Patty, are you okay? Say something?'

'Madam, are you quite all right?' begged Jermaine

Snapping myself back to the present, I blurted, 'It's him.'

Denial

'Robert Schooner?' Alistair repeated the name in disbelief. 'You think Robert Schooner is on board this ship right now?'

His question was aimed at me and I didn't like the tone he was using. 'How long ago did he escape?' I asked, my own tone bordering on impatient.

It was Lieutenant Deepa Bhukari who answered. 'Exactly four weeks today.'

'And how long ago did the sabotage attacks begin to occur?' I demanded.

Lieutenant Baker said, 'Just over two weeks, unless we count the burnt-out cabin of Isibaya Motene. Then it's exactly three weeks.'

They were beginning to get the picture. 'We are in Canadian waters now. Where was the Aurelia three weeks ago?' It was a rhetorical question because we all knew the ship left the Caribbean three weeks ago.

'How would he get on board?' argued the captain.

Giving him a deadpan expression, I admitted, 'I got on board dressed as a Jamaican woman with brown boot polish on my face and arms when the ship was in Madeira. Schooner had confined me to my cabin if you remember. With the help of … friends,' I elected to not name Barbie and Jermaine, 'and a little acting. I got on board without showing my passport and, truthfully, it was easy. Robert Schooner knows people on board. He had accomplices back then, who's to say we got them all when we caught him.'

Alistair took a moment to mentally note the need to review security measures but fired back with yet more argument. 'Why would he risk it? He escapes from prison but runs right back to a place where he is going to be recognised and recaptured. It's just him against all of us. He has the whole world to use as a refuge. He speaks about eight languages to varying degrees but is fluent in at least four of them. He could go anywhere.'

Speaking slowly to make my point clear, I said, 'But nowhere will give him the satisfaction of revenge.'

Alistair's shoulder slumped. 'You really think Robert Schooner is the saboteur.'

It was time to explain my rationale. With a glug of gin, my third because I needed them to calm my nerves, I started talking. 'The cabin that was firebombed belonged to a chef from Botswana. It looks like a terrible, possibly racially motivated, crime that has no tangible connection to the acts of sabotage that follow. Who was in it before her?'

Alistair gave me a blank look: he didn't know. There was no reason why he should, He was the captain of the entire ship with over two thousand five hundred crew. That no one else had thought to question it was sloppy.

I nodded to Barbie, who said, 'Shaun Metcalf.'

Alistair frowned and repeated the name. 'Shaun Metcalf. Shaun Metcalf. Why do I know that name?'

I knew it because it was indelibly inked into my memory. 'He was one of a pair of men who stole a priceless sapphire many years ago.' I made the statement and let it sink in. I'd already explained my theory to Barbie, Wayne, Sam, and Jermaine and I knew I was right.

Realisation dawned, not just on Alistair's face but on the faces of the security team too. Baker, Schneider, Bhukari ... they were all present when Commander Robert Schooner shot the captain and dived overboard.

Robert Schooner, the then deputy captain of the Aurelia, murdered Jack Langley and pinned the murder on me. Jack was the other man who stole the jewel, but when Shaun got caught and went to jail, Jack avoided prison by escaping with the jewel. Schooner planned to leave me rotting in a jail cell, take the sapphire, and vanish, but with luck, and the help of two people who became my very good friends, I avoided the hangman's noose and managed to uncover who really killed Jack Langley.

Alistair's eyes were staring far into the distance as he worked it out in his head, and when his eyes met mine, he nodded. 'He didn't know Shaun had left the ship,' I guessed. 'Shaun was just another patsy, but Robert wanted him dead for the sake of revenge. Robert knows this ship better than most and he came from engineering, much like Commander Ochi. He has the technical know how to do all the things he has done and more.'

'Did he know Commander Yusef?' asked Lieutenant Baker.

Alistair thought about that for a moment. 'I don't know. Robert had worked with me for years, but who's to say whether they worked together at some point in the past.'

'I made a mistake,' I admitted, getting people to look my way. 'Lieutenant Schneider told me Tomlinson was accused of possessing marijuana and that the deputy captain let him off when it came to his discipline hearing. It didn't occur to me that he meant a different deputy captain from Commander Yusef. If I had questioned it, I might have worked this out hours ago.'

Alistair paced to the window and turned to face the room, 'He has to have more planned. If this is revenge for foiling his attempt to get the sapphire, then this is about you and me,' he said, his eyes leaving no doubt that I was the *you* he referred to. 'He may have designs on other people in this room too. It was one of his biggest personality flaws; he was vindictive. When someone crossed him, he went after them and wouldn't stop until they begged him to.'

The captain's comment got a few knowing nods from the crew around the room and I remembered him firing both Barbie and Jermaine for assisting me. He'd threatened to ditch them at the next port, no matter where it was.

'He has Molly,' I stated. 'I think she is probably still alive. If he had killed her as part of his revenge upon me, he would have made it public, or done it in a way that would ensure I found out. I worry that he has something diabolical planned.'

'He probably does,' agreed Alistair wearily. 'If this is him, then the worst is yet to come.'

I wasn't done berating myself for not seeing it sooner. 'He used a kitchen knife,' I growled at myself. I'd been going back over what I'd seen in the last twenty-four hours, and now that I knew who was behind it, it all seemed so obvious. With everyone looking at me, I explained, 'He killed Jack Langley with a knife, stabbing him in the back in his cabin. Then he killed Lieutenant Davis by stabbing a kitchen knife through his ear. He likes to stab people and he always uses a kitchen knife. It was like signing his name when he stabbed Commander Yusef.'

I think Alistair wanted to tell me I was being too harsh on myself, but my outburst made him think. 'He wanted the uniform.' It was a bold statement and it needed to be expanded.

'What for, Alistair?'

He didn't turn his face to look at me, not straight away. He was trying to work something out.

The radios all crackled at the same time. 'Captain to the bridge. Captain to the bridge. This is Deputy Captain Ochi, requesting the captain to the bridge.'

With a deep frown because the transmission broke his concentration, Alistair lifted his radio and pressed the send button. 'This is the captain. You're on a secure channel. What is it?'

I think everyone in the suite held their breath. I know I didn't breathe as I waited for Commander Ochi to speak again. Whatever had occurred, he considered it too great a matter for him to deal with. As second in command of the ship, surely there could be few problems he couldn't handle himself, but then he'd only been elevated to that position a few hours ago, maybe he was still unsure of his bounds.

At the end other end, Ochi pressed the transmit button, but he didn't speak straight away. I heard him breathe, a huffing exhale like a terrified sigh before delivering terrible news. 'It's the missing woman, sir. I think we've found her.'

Terror on the High Seas

My body propelled itself from the couch with Anna in my arms. I couldn't breathe now if I wanted to. What was he going to say next? Was Molly's body so badly broken they couldn't be sure if it were her or not?

Alistair was already moving, a motion with his free hand getting all his lieutenants on their feet and hurrying toward the door. 'We're on our way, Ochi. ETA five minutes.'

I wasn't staying put, and I wasn't staying quiet. 'Is she alive?' I cried out to stop the captain in his tracks. He was almost at my door, his pace faltering as he paused to relay my question.

I could feel my heart hammering in my chest, listening for Commander Ochi's response. 'Yes. She's alive. I can see her.'

Relief washed through me, but Commander Ochi's reply hid something, and I could hear it in the way he answered. Also, he wanted us to come to the bridge, he ought to want us to go to Molly's location. 'Where is she,' I begged.

Ochi's reply chilled me to my bones. 'I can't tell.'

We all went; Barbie, Sam, and Jermaine around me for comfort and support as well as their own concern and we ran the whole way to the bridge elevator. There we had no choice but to pause, but we tapped our feet impatiently until the elevator doors swished open on the bridge level and ran through the passageways on the other side. Alistair shouted for anyone in the passageway to clear the path; he wasn't hanging around.

We burst into the ship's forward control room, the panoramic view which had always taken my breath away before, now of no interest as I looked around for Commander Ochi.

'This way, madam,' Jermaine nudged me to follow. I couldn't see Commander Ochi because he was standing close to a monitor screen and the people around him were all taller than he. They were spreading out to let Alistair in which was how I got to see his deputy. I also got a glimpse of the monitor screen and there was Molly. She looked terrified. There was no sound coming from the screen; wherever the feed was coming from, it provided picture only, but none of us needed to hear her to know she was screaming for help.

Tears were visible on her face, her mouth forming silent cries for help and we could all see why. I couldn't tell where she was, but whichever part of the ship Schooner chose to stash her in, it was filling with water.

Feeling sick, I couldn't stop myself from asking a question I already knew the answer to. 'Where is that?'

Commander Ochi looked wretched when he looked at me. 'We can't tell, Mrs Fisher. It is probably below the water line, but it could be a room with a watertight bulkhead door. A person would be able to push water in to replace the air inside and it would fill to the top before it found a way out.'

Slowly drowning with the certain knowledge that was your fate. If I thought I felt sick before, the wave of revulsion coursing through my body now almost ejected my lunch.

'We have to find her,' I stammered. Barbie was at my side, holding my arm as much for the support I gave her as that which she could give to me.

'Hey, that place looks familiar,' she snapped, letting go of me to edge closer. Those closest moved out of the way to let her get a better look. Molly was wearing a dress mercifully since the bottom half of her bikini was in an evidence bag. Where it had come from wasn't important. The only factor that mattered was her location.

Barbie swore. 'Where is it?' I begged her to tell me.

'I don't know,' she wailed. 'It looks really familiar, but I cannot figure out where I recognise it from.' Wherever it was, it was a small space and wouldn't take long to fill.

I turned to look up at the captain with imploring eyes. 'We have to find her, Alistair.'

Through gritted teeth, Alistair growled. 'We will.' It was a promise he couldn't make, not with the slightest degree of confidence, but I didn't challenge his statement. We all wanted this to end well and it would be no one's fault when it didn't. Except perhaps mine. I could have worked this out faster. I could have kept Molly safe, stopped her from going off by herself yesterday. Or maybe, I should have just lost to Schooner all those months ago. I would have gone to jail, my life essentially over, and no one would have mourned me.

'I don't know how they are in our feed. The monitor switched to show this without warning,' said Commander Ochi.

'It's Robert Schooner,' replied Alistair, his voice still a husky, angry growl. His statement got a lot of questioning looks for those who had not just come from my suite. Quickly, Alistair explained our thoughts, loudly enough that all could hear. When he finished and we could see they believed us, he said, 'Robert came from engineering, just like you, Commander Ochi. He has tapped into the ship's systems and could be listening in to every word we say.'

Loyalty and Deceit

'That's right, Alistair. I could be,' chuckled Robert Schooner, upon hearing what the Aurelia's captain had to say. They knew it was him now, which was a little disappointing, he'd hoped throwing them Tomlinson would keep them off his scent for a while. He could drop the Edward Smith name now at least. Or, rather, he could use it one last time, not so much for his own amusement, which was why he picked it in the first place, but for the shock effect it would create.

As he wiped away the last of the fake blood from his chest, he shook his head remembering how easy it had been to convince Tomlinson he was dying. A small amount of acting, a croaking, wheezing voice and the stupid steward believed Mashkov had stolen the loot and shot the former deputy captain. With a chuckle, he replied to Alistair's comment, 'It took you long enough to figure it out, old boy. Unfortunately, it's too late now.'

'Too late for what?' asked Lieutenant Mashkov.

Robert Schooner turned his attention toward the murderous young security officer. 'Ah, yes, Mashkov. I ought to tell you the final stage of the plan now it is at hand.' Mashkov had been one of his loyal men back when he was dethroned. The others he'd involved in his little plot to steal the sapphire and all the money Jack Langley had squirreled away over the years, were all caught, tried, and sentenced. Mashkov alone had been clever enough to evade their detection, or perhaps bright enough to see that Schooner was going to get caught and switched sides at the last moment. Whichever it was, Schooner sought him out when he escaped from jail. He needed help to get back onto the ship, and who better to provide that assistance than a greed-motivated member of the security team. Not only that, it meant he could get his hands on the swipe card and code he needed to get onto the bridge and had an armed man to call upon with access to other weapons.

Mashkov jumped at the chance to make a fortune when Schooner revealed he had stashed Jack Langley's money in his old cabin. Both Mashkov and Tomlinson believed him when he said it was behind a panel in the deputy captain's quarters. However, once he had it, his two accomplices had all but outlived their usefulness. He'd known Mashkov would kill Tomlinson when he told him to and that he would feel no remorse about helping him to lock a girl in a room with sea water being pumped into it.

Mashkov performed all his tasks, loyally, diligently, and faithfully because he thought he was going to get a huge financial reward. Unfortunately for Mashkov, loyalty and diligence were not the same as being clever, and he couldn't see that once he eliminated Tomlinson, his own death was Schooner's obvious next step.

That neither had been bright enough to question why he felt a need to sabotage the ship surprised Schooner. He'd prepared lies, because there was no way he could tell them the truth, but they never challenged him on it. Nor did they question his desire to be called Edward Smith or have a broad enough base of knowledge to recognise the name.

Jabbing his finger at Mashkov's sidearm, Schooner asked, 'That's the gun which killed that idiot Tomlinson? Can I see it?'

Obediently, Mashkov removed his issued sidearm and handed it over butt first.

Schooner shot him and placed the gun on the table.

The terrible noises Mashkov made as his blood seeped from the hole in his chest couldn't penetrate Schooner's focus. This was the end of the game now. He was ready to deal the final blow. However, he couldn't do it from where he was. He'd been hiding below decks all these weeks, but he'd made one successful trip to the bridge. Now it was time for another.

The final piece of his puzzle couldn't be achieved without a direct link to the ship's navigation computer and that meant he had to go right up to the control hub at the front of the superstructure.

One might be given to think this an impossible task. The bridge itself is filled with senior officers, all of them already on high alert, and they now knew he was behind the recent acts of sabotage. However, Robert Schooner had endured months in a cell awaiting his trial in St Kitts. Months where he could plot and plan and figure out how he would exact his revenge. How he would be able to achieve that which he wanted, right down to the minutest detail.

The girl was doing a marvellous job of distracting the crew. They would waste hours looking for her, and it didn't matter if they found her before she drowned or not, because Robert Schooner didn't need hours. He was going to be famous, that was for certain. His name would live in maritime history forever, just like Edward Smith.

Lights Out

I was trying to not be in the way as activity raged around us on the bridge. Barbie and Sam were with me still, but Jermaine had returned to the Windsor Suite. Wayne had been released from sickbay and wanted to join us. Jermaine would collect him.

Heated discussion abounded as teams stared at schematics, each of them dissecting the ship a deck at a time to identify possible spaces where Molly might be trapped. Through their radios, they coordinated the effort of teams of security guards as they ran from one possible point to the next, frantically eliminating them one by one. It was painstakingly slow.

Yet more of the crew, working with Commander Ochi, did their best to work out how Schooner was getting into their feed. He'd tapped into the monitor, but that wasn't all. Over the last few weeks, he'd shown he could get into the public address system, and the fire system to name just two. What else might he be able to access? The possibilities were as endless as they were terrifying.

I wanted a gin and tonic to settle my nerves but there was none to be had and I couldn't have stomached it anyway. The screen showing Molly was right there in front of me. I couldn't look at it, and I couldn't look away. Her calls for help had subsided, the camera positioned way up above her head showing the water level now around her knees as the compartment continued to fill. Occasionally, she moved about, looking for anything that she could use to help her situation, but the compartment looked to be devoid of anything useful.

In the next instant, the screen showing my terrified housemaid went blank. But it wasn't just the monitor screen that shut off. Everything in the bridge switched off in the same instant. Every computer, every television screen, every piece of equipment powered down at the same time. My eyes darted in every direction, trying to find a person with a master switch they had accidentally turned off. There wasn't one of course.

This was Schooner.

The air filled with expletives as around me men and women slapped the sides of their computers, begging them to return to life or simply sagged in their seats as they acknowledged the ramifications of this latest drama.

My eyes sought out Alistair. He looked shell-shocked. Watching him, I saw his lips flap a few times, opening and closing as he tried to find something to say, some order to give. His officers were all turning his way, bewildered by the latest turn of events. They were dumbfounded and wanted guidance that only he could provide.

One officer, a man in his late thirties wearing Lieutenant Commander's insignia, got right in front of the captain's face. 'The ship is drifting, sir! What are your orders?'

Alistair didn't react at all for a second, the notion of his ship being crippled perhaps too much to comprehend. Then his shoulder twitched as if it wanted to shrug but had been wrestled back under control, and I saw his jaw tighten. Just before the man could repeat his question, Alistair started barking orders.

'The bridge connection to the ship's controls has been severed, but there are redundancy systems for everything. He's shut us off and that must mean he is planning to operate the ship from inside the back-up control room. It's never been used to my knowledge but was included in the original design in case the bridge was ever to suffer a catastrophic failure. I believe this counts,' he injected a small smile to show he was being ironic. 'Some systems can also be controlled where they are fitted. Steering and engines to name just two. We can take control of the ship manually if that is what we need to do.' He pointed at two members of his security team. 'You two will remain here to advise me if the bridge comes back to life and to prevent anyone accessing it. I must warn you,' he raised his voice so all could hear, 'Robert Schooner may not be working alone. I cannot guess what insanity he may yet have planned, but this is our ship. This is our home. The people on board it are our guests, and we will protect them from harm no matter what form that harm might take.' He lifted his right hand to hold his radio aloft. 'We stay in radio contact. We find the girl. We find Robert Schooner, and we stop him. You know your jobs. Let's get to it.'

As his words died away, the silence which prevailed while he was speaking was replaced by a shout. 'Sir, the ship is changing course!' The call came from a young woman near the panoramic windows. I wondered how she could tell until I saw the large compass set into the console next to her. Schooner could cut off the power, but nothing shuts off the Earth's magnetic pull.

A hand went up, whipping into the air as across the bridge a man wearing headphones jumped to his feet. 'Sir, I cannot transmit. He's cut the feed from our antennae.'

Robert Schooner had cut the Aurelia off from the rest of the world and he had at least partial control of it. I didn't know much about how the ship works, but I knew everything was electronic, the signal from the controls here transmitted to a computer somewhere else and converted into mechanical movement of the rudder or whatever system had been instructed to perform an action.

Alistair clapped his hands together, a sharp noise to break the spell. 'Move people!' The brief silence vanished in a heartbeat as a hubbub of noise erupted. Everyone in the room started doing things all at once. Like an electric shock passing through the bridge, everyone was suddenly on their feet and moving. He was right, they had jobs to do and they knew how to do them.

Did that go for me too? What was my job? The answer echoed back inside my head: find and catch the bad guy. Biting my lip and wondering how I was going to do that, I watched Alistair's crew running from the bridge. They had fire in their bellies. They were all heading to the back-up control room, wherever that was. There, they would take control of the ship again. Is that where Schooner was located? Did he have a team of armed mercenaries waiting to repel the crew? What on Earth was his final goal?

The former deputy captain had managed to sow disruption and chaos. The security team were spread all over the ship, more than half of them engaged in the search for Molly together with other members of the crew, once again roped in to assist.

Feeling the familiar itch at the back of my skull, I shook off Barbie's grip, dodged around Sam and snagged Alistair before he too could run off to the back-up control room.

'Patricia,' he said my name as if remembering me for the first time in the last five minutes. 'I have to go. You should return to your suite and wait there. It will be safer for you to stay in one place with your friends.

'He's been drawing you out,' I blurted before the captain could escape. 'Your security team are spread thinly. Whatever he has planned, it is happening now. He took Molly to get at me, but also to create a diversion. Could he mount an attack? He already cut off your control of the ship. If he has barricaded himself in the backup control room, he then now has control. What if he is about to launch an attack and has a force of armed men on board? Could he hijack the entire ship? If he is steering and can cut off your communication with the outside world, he can take the ship wherever he wants. What if he has more people waiting to board once he has control?'

The horror of my suggestion was apparent on Alistair's face and on those around him who overheard my questions. It caused yet another pause in the people rushing from the bridge to carry out Alistair's orders. Grimly, the captain said, 'Lieutenant Schneider?'

'Yes, sir?'

'Take a squad of twelve to the armoury. Break out the assault rifles and be ready.'

I swallowed hard. I'd seen the ugly weapons the ship held just in case of ... whatever. The likelihood of pirates attempting to board a ship the size of Aurelia was almost inconceivable. Almost, but not quite, and for that fact, there was a stash of powerful weapons capable of far more damage than the standard handguns could hope to inflict. If Schooner had reinforcements on board, Alistair needed to be ready.

Schneider saluted his captain, gathering eleven volunteers or voluntolds swiftly. With a grim nod toward his friend Lieutenant Baker, he hurried from the bridge. Everyone else was decamping, just the two guards remaining behind so the bridge wasn't deserted and to report if the power returned.

Alistair wanted me to go to my suite, and though I had no desire to do so, I knew I would just be in the way if I followed him to the backup control room. Until someone found Molly, or I thought of something constructive I could do, I might as well gather in the suite with my friends. We could all fret together there.

What Sam Said

We had to wait to get an elevator, giving the bridge crew and security team priority: they all had jobs to do, we did not. I held Sam's hand, more to stop mine from shaking than because I thought he needed it.

'Do you think we will crash, Mrs Fisher?' Sam asked. The elevator was coming back up to get us, but the wait was killing me.

To make it easier on myself, I distracted my brain by answering his question. 'We can't crash, Sam, it's an ocean. There's nothing to crash into.'

His brow furrowed deeply as he thought about my answer. 'What about icebergs?'

The elevator pinged and a lightbulb came on in my head. Barbie moved forward, stepping into the elevator car, and Sam moved to follow her, his hand tugging mine when I didn't move. My eyes were open, but they weren't focussing on anything. I stayed that way long enough that Barbie had to put her arm out to stop the doors from closing again.

'Patty?' she prompted.

Wordlessly, I stepped forward, lost in thought as I tried to see the clues from a different standpoint. It was the scariest idea I could possibly imagine.

I swallowed hard. 'Barbie, do you remember when we talked about what the worst thing the saboteur could be planning might be?'

'Yeah,' she replied cautiously. 'Jermaine said he might try to cripple the ship. It looks like his prediction came true.'

I bit my lip and shook my head. 'But we're not crippled, are we? The ship is under power and being steered. It's just not being steered by anyone on the crew.'

'What are you saying, Mrs Fisher?' asked Sam.

I genuinely didn't want to articulate my thoughts, as if saying them might somehow make them come true. 'I think he plans to sink the ship.' My words came out at a volume barely above a whisper, but from the reaction they received, I might as well have shouted them.

Barbie's hands flew to her face in horror. I didn't know that I was right, but it felt right. Over three weeks, Robert Schooner had slowly infiltrated the ship's delicate electronic systems. The sabotage the crew saw came as a result of that, either as a side-effect of his tampering, or a distraction to hide what he was doing. Now, he had control of the ship and could kill everyone on board.

The elevator reached the top deck a hundred feet or more beneath the bridge itself. The doors opened to let us out and I rushed along the passageway and around the corner to the nearest window. There I looked to the ocean outside. There were icebergs everywhere, too small to do any damage, I hoped. These were just tiddlers, but how long would it take for him to find the one that would put a hole in the ship.

The moment I thought that, a clanging noise reverberated through the ship and I felt the deck vibrate.

'Oh, God,' gasped Barbie. 'We just hit something.'

There were other passengers around, but not many; this wasn't a part of the ship where they could find anything to look at or do. A pair of joggers went past, concerned looks on their faces as they too wondered what might have caused the noise they just heard.

'The captain's uniform!' I snapped, slapping my forehead with an open palm. 'How could I be so blind?'

Sam got in front of me. 'What is it, Mrs Fisher?' Barbie's wide eyes were turned in my direction also, waiting for me to explain my outburst.

'He's going to dress as the captain and ride the ship to the ocean bed. He got everyone off the bridge so he could be on it.' My feet were already moving, picking up speed as I started running back toward the bridge.'

Barbie caught up to me just as I rounded the corner, but there all three of us stopped in our tracks.

Robert Schooner was bathed in light coming from the open elevator doors. He saw me at the same moment I saw him, but unlike me, he was armed. I watched his right arm rise as if it was moving in slow motion. I had the time to take in the detail of the pristine white uniform he wore - it was adorned with captain's insignia – and the fresh pink scar on his face. I didn't know what might have befallen him to cause the scar, but as I looked at the expression of pure rage on his face, it never once occurred to me to duck or run. In his left hand was a bag which he dropped to the floor, freeing the hand to support the weapon held in his right.

Barbie was screaming something, shoving Sam back down the passageway we had just emerged from, but my feet weren't moving. Seeing Robert Schooner again was like seeing a ghost. He created me in many ways. Forcing me to work out who was behind Jack Langley's murder unearthed a skillset I didn't know I possessed. If he hadn't tried to frame me for murder, I would have left the ship in Madeira, crawled back to my cheating husband, and returned to my life cleaning houses for pennies. Despite that, he haunted my dreams more regularly than any of the other killers I'd encountered and now he was staring right at me.

The first shot jolted my thoughts, breaking the spell as the bullet slammed into the bulkhead behind me.

'Patty!' Barbie's scream came from behind me. I knew I was supposed to be running away now, but my feet still wouldn't move. Other people were screaming; there were passengers in the passageway behind him. They ran in the opposite direction, fleeing for their lives as Schooner lined up to take another shot.

I could see his finger tightening on the trigger again, but I didn't get to see him finish the move because I was suddenly moving through the air. Bodily shunted out of the path of the next bullet, and then yanked back to safety down the passageway where Sam and Barbie hid, I fell to the carpet and found Jermaine looming over me.

Another shot rang out, but there were no footsteps running toward us, and the passageway was silent. Jermaine snuck a glance around the corner, darting his head out and snatching it back lest a bullet fly his way. None came and he relaxed visibly, turning to face the three of us, 'That was Schooner, wasn't it?'

Sam giggled. 'He shot at us. That was fun! Wait till I tell mum!'

'Don't you dare, Sam Chalk,' I begged. 'Your poor mother would have a heart attack.' I had ended up on the carpet, but a hand from Jermaine got me back to my feet. 'Yes, Jermaine, that was the former deputy captain at his murderous best. He's on the bridge now and I think he plans to sink the ship. We must get the captain and the security team back here. He's pulled a double bluff, cutting the power to get them all off the bridge but only so he could take it for himself.'

'There are two guards up there,' Barbie gasped. 'We have to warn them!'

I didn't disagree but I didn't have a radio. None of us did. 'Where's Wayne?' I asked, making my way cautiously back to the bridge elevator.

Jermaine said, 'I believe he is more badly hurt than he is letting on, madam. Dr Davis gave him some pain medication and whatever it was must be quite strong because he fell asleep on the couch. I considered waking him, but he looked so peaceful.' My butler explained all this in the time it took us to confirm Schooner had gone up to the bridge.

'I'll run for help,' said Barbie, breathlessly. 'There must be someone with a radio nearby!' her voice was already fading into the distance as the lithe athlete sprinted away, but she only got twenty yards before a pair of security guards burst through a set of double doors on their way to us. They probably didn't hear the shots Schooner took but they would have heard the reports from the terrified passengers as they ran from him.

Barbie quickly reversed direction, running ahead of the ship's security as they came to us. 'Quickly! I shouted, somewhat needlessly as they were already running flat out. 'It's Schooner! He's gone up to the bridge. You have to warn the two men the captain left up there!' I recognised the two men in their white uniforms, but I didn't know their names, and this wasn't the time for introductions.

They were both on their radios, one trying to raise the two men left on the bridge, the other trying to raise Commander Ochi, the captain or anyone else who might be able to respond.

'This is Commander Ochi,' his voice cut over the airwaves. He was speaking quickly but maintained his calm. 'You say former Deputy Captain Robert Schooner has shot at passengers and is now on the bridge?'

'That's correct, sir. There are no casualties that we know of,' replied the guard talking to him. The other guard was still trying to raise the two men left behind in the bridge, but he couldn't get an answer from them.

Commander Ochi said, 'We are on our way to you. Do not wait for us. You must ascend to the bridge now and stop him. Use deadly force if necessary but go now!'

It was a terrible order to give, the two men exchanged a grim glance but advanced on the elevator without hesitation. Schooner would hear the elevator coming and be able to start laying bullets into it before they could even get the doors open. We knew it, Commander Ochi knew it, and the two men now summoning the elevator knew it. Their companions on the bridge were most likely already dead, caught unawares by a man approaching them in uniform. He would get the drop on them, and if he did plan to sink the ship, he wouldn't care about how many he killed along the way.

I couldn't think of anything to say, but before any one of us could say anything to the two men about to embark on what felt like a suicide mission, it became obvious something was wrong.

'The elevator isn't moving,' said the one who had been speaking to Commander Ochi. He pressed his ear to the doors, perhaps hoping to hear the distant rumble of the car moving but brought his head away again with an angry expression. 'He's disabled it,' he observed, sounding both angry and relieved at the same time.

I didn't want to watch the two men leave in the elevator because I feared I would never see them alive again, but this was worse.

The sound of fast feet brought my eyes around as two dozen white uniforms burst through the same doors the first two had less than a minute ago.

'The elevator is disabled,' Sam shouted, always wanting to be included and be helpful. His announcement came just as those running towards us began to slow, the news wasn't well received.

A senior man, another Commander, pushed his way to the front and jabbed the elevator call button as if he might have the magic touch. More crew arrived, and some passengers, who were escorted away politely, but nothing happened until Alistair's voice rang out. He was coming through the doors and he looked ready to chew through steel.

'It's definitely him?' he asked, sounding like he wasn't really ready to believe it until now.

His question was aimed at his crew, but I stepped forward to answer because none of his crew had seen Robert Schooner, only me and my friends had. 'It's really him, Alistair. He shot at me and I think he plans to sink the ship.' I knew it was a bold statement to make and it prompted a range of different expressions from the crew looking my way. Some were terrified that I might be right, others clearly thought I was nuts, but Alistair didn't bother to question me.

He raised his right hand, pressing the transmit button on his radio as he brought it to his lips. 'Robert, this is Alistair.'

No one said anything. I'm not sure some of them were even breathing as we all waited to see if Schooner would answer. Seconds ticked by, then a crackle preceded the sound of a voice I never expected to hear again. 'Good afternoon, Alistair. I'm afraid Robert isn't here today. My name is Edward Smith.'

Alistair's eyes flared, as around him Schooner's statement was met with confusion, or horror depending on whether the person recognised the name or not.

It was Barbie who spoke first, slipping her hand into Jermaine's and moving into his personal space when she said, 'Who is Edward Smith?'

Someone sobbed, a man somewhere tucked at the back of the crowd of crew silently waiting to see what would happen now.

Alistair lowered his radio, his eyes flicking to the ceiling and then back down. He looked right into my eyes and said, 'Edward Smith was the captain of the Titanic.'

Assault the Bridge

A chill passed through the passageway we occupied, whispers and muttering breaking out between a dozen people or more in different pockets, but they all stopped again when Alistair raised his radio once more.

'That's fascinating, Robert. But if you succeed in sinking this ship, you will die too. What do you gain?'

Robert Schooner chuckled into the radio. 'Vengeance, dear fellow. I am now the captain of this ship, as it always should have been. I sent a message before I shut off the ship's communication array. The world will learn of the last fateful transmission the Aurelia made before it vanished beneath the icy waves with everyone on board. It will be the biggest commercial shipping disaster in the history of the world, outstripping even the Titanic because of me. Because Robert Schooner claimed his rightful captaincy and took the ship to the bottom of the ocean where it belongs. The conspiracy and conjecture that will follow the story of the Aurelia's sinking will go on forever. Shrouded in mystery, my name will be the one they remember, yours will be a by-line, and Patricia Fisher will be forgotten forever. You may think that aiming at icebergs is a haphazard way of sinking the ship, but don't worry, I've fitted explosives all along the inside of the hull. If the icebergs fail to do the job, I'll press the detonator in my hand. The same goes for any attempt to stop me. If I think you are trying to get to me on the bridge, I'll blow out the bottom of the ship. Now, if you'll excuse me, there are tasks to which I must attend. It's been fun chatting with you, Alistair. Truthfully, I wanted to kill you in person, to drive a knife deep into your gut and watch your face as you finally accept the futility and pointlessness of your existence. I shall settle for knowing you went down with the ship. As will I, Alistair, sitting in the captain's chair as the ship descends beneath the waves.' The hiss of background noise from his radio stopped as he let go of his send button.

He'd said his piece and we knew what he planned to do. The only question now was what could we do about it?

A fight broke out, two men shoving each other as they argued about whether we should start for the lifeboats.

'Nobody touches the lifeboats,' commanded Alistair, his voice like steel. 'The passengers are already spooked enough. He duped us. He duped me; I should say. The back-up control room was a red herring, a lure to get us out of the bridge, and I fell for it hook, line, and sinker. He killed Yusef because he knew Ochi would move up to be my deputy and that would mean his eyes were no longer attuned to the ships engineering systems. That is a mistake I have already corrected. Ochi will work out what Schooner has done. He will wrestle the ship back under our control, but that may take some time. We will give him that time. I am going to assault the bridge.'

'But Schooner said he would blow up the ship if he thought we were trying to stop him,' Lieutenant Baker pointed out.

Alistair agreed, 'Yes. He also said he was going to sink us anyway. I think he is bluffing about the explosives. How would he get them on board?'

'How has he done any of this?' argued another man. 'What if he has rigged the hull to blow?'

'Then he has the power to sink us and intends to do so no matter whether we obey his instructions or not. I, for one, choose to fight. There will be no order to join me, but anyone ...'

'I'm in, sir,' snapped Lieutenant Schneider, leaping with both feet, and only just beating Baker and Bhukari to it. Their shouts were echoed by every crew member present, even those who were not part of the security detachment stepped up to join the fight.

'How are you going to get up to the bridge?' I begged to know, shocked at all that was happening and failing to understand how they would stop him before he smashed a hole in the ship. To punctuate my thoughts, another jarring thud echoed through the ship and caused the deck to vibrate.

Alistair took a pace forward, closing the gap between us, and reached out to put a hand on my arm. 'Like every other elevator on the planet, there is a set of stairs next to it. They are also access protected by a code and swipe card combination, and there is a ladder running up each side of the structure on the outside. In addition, there is an observation area right on top of the structure with a hatch. The door on the hatch, and those on the side doors all open from the inside, so we will have to employ some explosives to force our way inside.'

'Do you have explosives?' I blurted my question, terrified by what was being proposed.

'We have some,' Alistair replied calmly, showing how even his nerves were and reminding me why I fell into his bed the first time. 'These are drastic measures, but Robert Schooner has left us no choice.' He raised his voice to address the men and women around him. 'We will assault the bridge and take back this ship. Tonight, we will toast our success with champagne and the name Robert Schooner will be forgotten forever.' He held my gaze for a moment, offered me a tight nod of his head, and then began to hand out instructions, breaking the group into squads with different tasks.

My feet were rooted to the spot, until I spotted Jermaine among one of the assault groups. His butler's coat was gone, discarded somewhere as he got ready to join in the fight to reclaim the ship. I started to move forward but Barbie moved to block my path.

'I have to stop him,' I wailed at her. 'What if he gets hurt?'

Quietly, she replied, 'What if any of them get hurt? I'm going too, Patty. I was crew once, I can help.'

Her announcement drove a spear of panic into my heart. Robert Schooner would be expecting this, I was certain of it. He was always one step ahead. I only beat him last time through blind luck and with help from Barbie and Jermaine. They would be walking into a trap, he planned to kill everyone on board, the bag I saw in his free hand was filled with weapons or explosives, I just knew it. They might beat him, and they had no choice other than to try, but how many of them would die in the attempt?

But as I thought that, I thought about how he was always one step ahead. Whatever we predicted he would do; he had already done it by the time we figured it out. As the familiar itchy feeling invaded the back of my skull, a calm began to settle over me. There were clues I had seen which I hadn't yet had time to investigate and as I ran them through my head, a feeling like electricity coursing through my veins made me gasp.

Like a possessed person, I reached around to grab Sam's hand. 'We have to go,' I blurted. Then to Barbie, I shouted. 'You need to come with me. I need your help, I need a radio, and I need to check something.'

I started to run, pulling Sam along behind me. It made Barbie chase after me with her questions. 'What things, Patty? What do you need to check? What's the radio for?'

I threw her a wicked smile, this one intended to make me look like a shark going after a swimmer. 'He thinks he has us beaten, Barbie. I need the radio because I'm going to threaten him.'

Barbie had been ready to join the force preparing to storm the bridge; curiosity, and the sense that I might be onto something, dictated she follow me instead. 'Where are we going, Patty?' she begged to know.

I made a show of checking my watch. 'It's gin o'clock, sweetie, we're going back to the Windsor Suite. We just have to make a quick detour first.'

'Detour?' she repeated incredulously.

Running along the passageway, my two companions just behind me, I had to turn my whole body to catch Sam's eye. 'Sam have you ever had a gin and tonic?'

His eyebrows rose an inch. 'No, Mrs Fisher. Mum doesn't often let me have alcohol. She says it makes me silly.' I guess I understood where Melissa was coming from, nevertheless, when this was over, it would be time for a gin. Right now, it was also time to speak to Robert Schooner, although first, I wanted Agent Garrett. He was armed and that might prove invaluable. I should have asked someone from the security team to come with us, but I only thought about that after we ran away from them. Now time was too tight.

Anna and Georgie rushed over to meet us as we came into the suite, wagging their tails excitedly and probably hoping for a gravy bone. I picked them both up to fuss them, feeling bad they had been left alone for several hours today, and carried them to the kitchen where I deposited them on the countertop and found them a treat.

Passing through the suite I realised Agent Garrett wasn't on the couch as expected. He wasn't anywhere in the suite, a quick check revealed, and with the communications knocked out by Schooner my phone wouldn't work either. 'So much for armed back up,' I murmured, pushing the problem to one side, and moving on.

Back in the kitchen I found Barbie. She was overflowing with questions. 'Patty, you need to tell me what is going on. You said Schooner is going to sink the ship. The ship feels like it is picking up speed and he is at the helm. Pretty soon, he's going to put a hole in the ship, but you wanted to come back to the suite. What are you up to? And why did we just go outside to mess with one of the lifeboats?'

'We didn't mess with a lifeboat, sweetie, we very deliberately released the anchor clamp that holds it in place. Do you know what happens when someone undoes the anchor clamp?'

'Yes,' she frowned. 'It sends a signal to the bridge so someone from the crew has to go to the lifeboat and perform a full check ...' her words tailed off as she saw what I was doing.

I shot her a smile, picked up the radio, cleared my throat and pressed the send button. 'Hello, Robert. Did you miss me?'

I wasn't sure he would answer but I was sure he would be listening. He would want to hear what the crew were saying. My guess, in fact, was that he'd been listening in for weeks, staying ahead of the ship's security team by knowing where they were and what they were doing. I paused my brain for a moment as my skull itched again – he had someone on the inside. I nodded to myself. That would explain how he got on board and how he came to have a gun. It might even explain how he got hold of the captain's uniform because he wouldn't want to show his face until it was absolutely necessary. Tomlinson – the name popped into my head – the steward was working for him or with him.

I didn't get to consider it any further because his voice filled the room. 'Patricia Fisher, what a terrible displeasure it was to see you again. I will be smiling broadly as the dark ocean closes over me, secure in the knowledge I will be ridding the planet of your menace.'

I chuckled at him; the last thing he expected. 'I'm afraid not, Robert. You're too late to kill me. Oh, I expect I will get a little cold, but rescue will be along in a few hours. If you check, you'll find crew outside carefully letting one of the lifeboats go. The ship may go down, and you can ride it to the bottom, but I won't be on it. Nor will my friends. You managed to kill my housemaid, well done.' I forced myself to sound unbothered by it. I pictured him rushing to the sides of the bridge to look down. He wouldn't be able to see all the lifeboats from there, but he would see the warning light on whichever console displayed it. No reply came for three or four seconds, but I wasn't going to fill the void he was leaving. In my head he was checking to see if I was telling the truth.

The faint crackle of the radio connecting heralded his voice growling at me. 'You think you can evade my vengeance, Patricia Fisher? You have no idea how wrong you are. There is no way to escape me.' His transmission ended abruptly, and with a sense of finality.

My shaking right hand replaced the radio on the kitchen countertop, and I looked up to find Barbie staring at me. Her lips were puffed out and her eyes narrowed as she tried to work out what I was up to. 'I'm not sure how that is going to help, Patty. He still has control of the ship. He's still going to find a giant iceberg and ram us into it or get bored and set off the explosives.'

I blew a hard breath out through my nose. 'If he has rigged the ship with explosives there is nothing we can do. We must assume his plan is to escape and he won't risk setting off the charges until he is clear.

Sam was likewise confused by my actions. 'I thought he said he was going down with the ship.'

I started for the door again. 'I'll explain on the way. I think I know where Molly is. We should get to her and then worry about Schooner.'

'Are we taking the dogs, Mrs Fisher?' asked Sam. Always looking to be helpful, he was offering to get their leads and collars.

'You know what? I think we should,' I shot him an encouraging smile.

I went to run to the door, but Barbie blocked my path. 'You do this Patty,' she complained. 'You do this thing where you have a master plan, but you don't tell any of us what it is. It can be ... irritating. It's like you think that if you share it, it won't work, or something.'

I dipped my head and gave her a sort of half shrug. 'Something like that, yes.'

She pursed her lips and folded her arms. 'Well, Patricia,' I couldn't remember the last time she called me anything other than Patty, 'I'm not leaving this suite until you tell me something. I want to know what is going on.'

Sam copied her, folding his arms, and moving to stand beside the athletic blonde woman. 'Yeah, me too, Patricia.'

I looked at them both with a smile on my face, my laughter barely contained because my assistant Sam was just so funny. Barbie couldn't keep her face straight either, a laugh bursting from her lips even as she tried to keep it inside.

'I'll let you into a little secret,' I told them both, mirth making it hard to talk. 'There's no one on the bridge.'

Ambush

Sam and Barbie followed me when I darted around them and ran to the door. I felt convinced I knew where I would find Molly and I needed to get there as fast as I could. I wanted to use the radio to call for assistance, but I couldn't tell anyone what I was up to without letting Robert Schooner also know. It was just us, but with help or without it, we needed to hurry.

I had both Anna and Georgie on their leads, my tiny sausage dogs leading the way. Barbie kept pace easily. 'Patty, what do you mean there's no one on the bridge? You saw Schooner going up in the elevator. The guards have all the stairwells covered, so he has to still be up there.'

'Except he isn't,' I stated, already getting out of breath.

'So he isn't planning to sink the ship?' Sam queried. He was no more able to follow my logic than Barbie.

Running to the elevators, we came across passengers in the passageway and had to fall silent: talking about sinking wouldn't be well received. Seeing people nonchalantly strolling the deck demonstrated how little the vacationers noticed. The ship was going faster than normal, but they couldn't tell that, I doubted many could, and they were going about their day as if nothing untoward were occurring.

Once we were well past them, I replied to Sam's comment. 'Oh, he's trying to sink the ship all right. He wants the world to believe he was on the bridge when it went down, that was the purpose of the transmission he sent, to make sure everyone would know where and when he died.' Barbie and Sam were looking at me with uncomprehending eyes. We got to the nearest bank of elevators, pressed the call button, and I breathlessly did my best to explain. 'He escaped from jail, so he is a wanted man. There are only two ways to stop the bounty hunters and law enforcement agents from trying to find him: get caught or die. He has chosen to die, but only in a virtual sense. If the world thinks he went down with the ship, no one will look for him.'

Another clang sent a vibration through the deck and some passengers walking by were looking concerned as they argued about what might be causing it.

Barbie leaned close to whisper, 'That was much bigger. He must be doing some damage to the ship.'

The elevator doors opened, my dogs scampering inside to almost trip those trying to get out. Safely inside, I stabbed the button for deck eight and continued my story. 'He wants me dead, you too probably, Barbie, and certainly Alistair, but he has gone to extreme lengths to get his revenge and I don't think that is what motivated him to come back to the ship. I think killing us is a by-product. He came back for the money.'

Sam's brow wrinkled. 'What money?'

Barbie likewise frowned at me. 'Yeah, Patty, what money?'

I smiled like the Cheshire cat and delivered the line that summed all this up, 'The money he hid behind the panel in the deputy captain's quarters.'

Barbie's mouth opened to argue, or possibly to ask me a question, but she closed it again.

Sam said, 'I didn't know they found any money.' He'd listened to Baker list all the evidence, or rather lack thereof, in Commander Yusef's cabin, and he was right that money was never mentioned.

'That's because Schooner had already taken it. He risked going all the way up to the bridge to kill Commander Yusef. We've been thinking it was because he wanted Commander Ochi out of his engineering role where he might have spotted what Schooner was doing, but I think Yusef's death was accidental or, at least, unplanned. Schooner came back to the ship to get the money he stole from Jack Langley. Barbie you must remember that he had several of the security team working for him at the time.'

'Yeah,' she snorted. 'They tried to kill us more than once.'

'They also controlled the crime scene in Jack Langley's cabin. Schooner was after the sapphire, but it wasn't there. What he found was most likely cash and other items: Langley had been stealing from rich widows and the like for months while on board. He stashed the goods in his own cabin, planning to retrieve them once he had the sapphire. He never got the sapphire and never had the chance to go back for the things he took from Jack Langley. However, it was worth enough for him to come back for it now. Sinking the ship is how he plans to get cleanly away. If he truly planned to go down with the ship, why would he bother to retrieve whatever was behind that panel? He has told the world where he is. Now he needs to escape with the money, leaving the world to believe his corpse was at the bottom of the ocean along with everyone else.'

'But some people would get off in the lifeboats,' argued Sam.

Barbie wrinkled her lips. 'That depends how big the hole is. If he finds the right iceberg ... plus any other ship would stop forward motion and activate the pumps, Schooner won't do either thing. The Aurelia could vanish beneath the waves in a matter of minutes. Even sooner if he really has got explosives rigged to the hull.'

'It won't matter if some people survive,' I argued. 'Their tale will just add to the mystery. Anyway, Schooner isn't on the bridge.'

Barbie was going to ask me to explain how he got off it when all the exits from it are blocked, but the elevator stopped to let someone on.

Wouldn't you know it? When the doors opened, Verity Tuppence was waiting outside with Rufus.

Rufus leapt forward with an excited bark, yanking Verity's arm to pull her off balance. She staggered forward into the elevator car as Rufus did his best to make knots out of the leads.

'Goodness!' she exclaimed, pitching forward when her feet got caught in the mess of dogs. Only Sam grabbing her arm to keep her upright stopped her from colliding with me. 'Oh, thank you, young man,' she said, getting her balance once more. 'Rufus you are such a naughty boy.'

I didn't think Rufus cared one bit what Verity thought, he was much too busy investigating Anna. The doors closed again, the car descending once more. I hadn't finished explaining about Schooner and now I couldn't. Not until Verity got off.

'What deck do you want?' asked Barbie, keen to lose our unexpected guest and hear the rest of what I had to say.

For a moment, Verity looked surprised by the question as if she didn't know the answer, but found her tongue to say, 'Where are you all going? It looks like you are going for a walk,' she observed, aiming her eyes at the dogs. 'Is it okay if I tag along? Rufus could do with some canine company and maybe I can learn some tricks from you to make him more obedient.'

She sounded so hopeful, like a person desperately in need of a friend, yet despite how rude it would seem, I needed to turn her down flat.

'We're off to rescue our friend who has been trapped in a sealed container that is being flooded by a maniac!' cheered Sam, too excited to contain himself.

'He's just joking,' I tried with a smile, hoping I could bluff away his outburst, but Verity wasn't buying a word of it.

Her free hand went to her mouth. 'Oh, my goodness. Is this something to do with the bangs and vibrations we've been feeling? My Vernon says the ship is going faster. I told him he was imagining things, but ... what's going on? You're Patricia Fisher, do we really have a maniac on board?'

How was I going to get out of this one now?

I decide to just lie. 'There was a malfunction, I believe. I'm a passenger here, just the same as you, Verity. I don't have a special inside line on what goes on with the crew. I did speak to the captain though, just in passing, and he said it was a minor electrical thing.' I was getting into my story now, making it up as I went along and adding layers because I thought they made it sound more convincing. 'Actually, he explained exactly what had happened, I just didn't understand it. It was far too technical for my brain. He told me the clanging noises are small icebergs, but they're nothing to worry about.' I hoped that part was true.

'They sure sound like something I should worry about,' replied Verity, sounding worried. She expected me to say something more, but my lie filled in the time we needed for the elevator to make it to deck eight.

'This is us,' I announced gamely, strutting forward, and tugging my dogs along with me.

'Ha!' said Verity. 'You're up to something. I think I'll tag along and see what it is. This cruise has been nowhere near as exciting as I thought it would be until now.' She sounded excited at the prospect of whatever it was we were doing, and as I rounded to face her, intending to order her to go away, I realised that she reminded me of me. A few months ago, I was a bored housewife, unaware that the thing missing from my life was a little intrigue and adventure. I wasn't going to rudely shoo her away, but I did need to warn her.

'All right, Verity. There is a maniac on board. We are not trying to catch him though; we are trying to rescue a person trapped in a container that is slowly filling with water. It's not far now, just be alert for a tall man with a scar on his face and gun in his hand.'

She put a hand to her chest. 'Do you think we will see him?'

I pursed my lips and started running, calling over my shoulder as I went, 'I sure hope not! Your only sensible course of action is to go back to your cabin and find a movie to watch. You're not going to do that though, are you?'

She sounded out of breath when she shouted back. 'It sounds boring compared to what you are doing.' We were leaving Verity and Rufus behind, but I couldn't slow my pace for her.

Barbie, right by my side, asked, 'Patty. Why are we on deck eight?'

Even after months of going running with Barbie, I was still a woman in her fifties who hadn't kept her fitness up. I was fitter than I was when I met her, vastly fitter, but speaking was a little more effort than I wanted to expend while also running as fast as I could. Knowing we were nearly there I slowed my pace to a walk and tried to get air back into my lungs.

After a few deep breaths, I managed to wheeze, 'He's got the money, he thinks the ship is on a collision course with a giant iceberg that will sink the ship, and he thinks Alistair and the ship's security team are still trying to get onto the bridge to stop him. His next move is to escape, leaving everyone to die while he slips away.

'Wait,' said Barbie. 'How is he getting off the ship? In fact, how did he even get off the bridge?'

'Is he going to swim to shore?' asked Sam.

'Truthfully, I haven't worked that out yet. My focus is on finding Molly.' I turned a corner, my memory serving me well to deliver me back to the place I needed to go. Pausing, I asked Barbie, 'Do you remember where Edgar Thomas was murdered?'

'Yes,' she replied, her voice curious to hear what I had to say next. 'He was on deck two, close to the elevators.'

I shook my head. 'No, that was where he was found. He was murdered here.' I led them around the corner where the deck eight water sports centre dominated our view. 'We are almost directly above the point where Edgar was found. Schooner killed him – I don't think he intended to – like Yusef, it happened because Edgar came across Schooner and he couldn't be allowed to live.'

Verity gasped. 'You talk about murder as if it were an everyday event.' She was bent double and using a hand against the bulkhead to keep herself upright.

I didn't want to respond to that. 'Edgar was found six decks below the water sports centre. What was he doing there? They didn't find where he was killed because they never thought to look in here. It's closed, isn't it? The weather and conditions do not allow for the ship to drop anchor as it might in the Caribbean. The jet skis, kayaks, and paddleboards are all put away, but they must require some maintenance which is what brought Edgar here. I think this is where Schooner has stashed Molly.'

'It has a fresh water supply for cleaning the equipment off,' said Barbie, then her face lit up as she put two and two together and realised that she did recognise the chamber Molly was in.

'She's in the decompression chamber!' we both squealed together.

I wanted to look here because in hours of searching below the passenger decks, the search parties hadn't found her and the number of possible places to fill with water had to be finite. It was only when I thought of Edgar Thomas again that it dawned on me to consider where he worked and not where he was found. The search parties had all been looking for Molly in the bottom six decks. The water sports centre on deck eight was possibly the only place above the crew area that she could be.

Barbie, a former water sports coach, entered the code for the door and swung it open.

'Cor, boats!' said Sam, taking in the dinghies, ribs, jet skis, and other seagoing equipment. Passengers could participate in many different activities if they so chose. Everything from scuba, hence the decompression chamber just in case, to snorkelling and trying their hand at spear fishing. The ship's equipment extended all the way up to jet skis and water skis where they would be towed by a member of the crew in a rib. I ignored it all as I darted across the room to the decompression chamber. I didn't know if it had ever been used to save a person, but it was being used right now to drown my housemaid.

A long hose snaked across the deck from a tap on the wall and up into the top of the chamber where I imagined it had been forced into a jammed-open valve. I yelled for Sam to turn off the tap and ran to the chamber with Barbie.

'How do we get it open?' I squealed, desperate to find Molly and find out if we were in time or too late. There was a window on the front through which we could see only darkness. I couldn't tell if I was looking at water or an empty chamber, until something fleshy swished by.

Molly was still treading water inside!

Barbie yelled, 'Stand back!' as she grabbed the handle, wound it around, and pulled. It didn't move, not at first, the water inside created a vacuum of sorts, but a tiny trickle of water around the edge of the door gave us a half second of warning before the weight pushing against the door from the inside thrust it outwards.

It looked like a giant washing machine emptying as the round door was flung open. A torrent of water sprang from within. The wave almost got both of my dachshunds, my reflexes saving them as I snatched them both into the air at the last moment. It meant I got soaked, the wave crested right around my nethers, and Barbie was almost washed away, only staying where she was because she had hold of the door handle still. On the other side of the room Sam and Verity got away with wet feet. However, from the centre of the swirling vortex washed Molly, emerging out of control, with a terrified scream, and an explosion of expletives. She bounced on the hard deck and got washed along it, tumbling and rolling, bedraggled but very much alive.

Barbie and I rushed to her, Anna and Georgie dumped roughly on the deck as I ran to check Molly's condition.

'Where are they!' Molly yelled. 'I'll kill 'em! I've been in there for hours. I've got wrinkles on my wrinkles.' She was more angry than anything else. I could see she was shivering with cold, but her dominant thought was to get her own back on those who put her in there. She said them, meaning it was plural persons.

'Molly are you all right?' I asked her, putting a hand on her shoulder.

She looked at me, then glanced at Barbie, seeing for the first time who had come to her rescue. 'Mrs Fisher? How did you find me?'

'That doesn't matter,' I assured her. 'We can go through that later. Are you all right?'

'I'm wet,' she complained. 'I think I probably ruined Jackson's dress. I guess I'm cold too. Did you catch them?'

'Them who?' asked Barbie, grabbing Molly's shoulder to get her attention. 'Who put you in there?'

Molly's lip curled as anger ruled her face again. 'Harry and Nicholai.' She called them several unprintable names. 'They just did what Edward Smith said. He is their boss and he is really creepy.'

'Yes, I am, aren't I?' said Robert Schooner, coming through the door of the water sports centre with a pistol in his hand.

Frozen Vengeance

He slammed the door shut, the clanging sound jolting me to restart my heart. My stomach was a heavy ball of fear that made me want to vomit. His gun was pointed squarely at me, but when Sam took a pace to his side, Schooner twitched his arm and shot a round in his direction.

Sam's hand went over his ears to protect them from the deafening noise in the closed steel compartment.

The gun swung back in my direction where Barbie, Molly, and I were huddled together. 'This is how you plan to escape,' I said, nodding to myself as I saw the truth of it. I should have seen it before now. 'Will you take a dingy or a rib? I asked. 'We've been hugging the coast. It can't be more than ten miles to get to shore. You could do that in either vessel.'

He smiled at me. 'It pains me to say it, but you are quite intuitive. I thought it was just luck when you linked me to Jack Langley and found the sapphire.' He motioned to Sam with the muzzle of his gun. 'Move over there with them.'

Sam didn't hesitate to do so, scurrying across the wet deck to get to us. I didn't want Schooner to see me looking, but Verity was still over that side of the room somewhere. If I squinted into the dark spaces between the equipment racks, he might follow my gaze and find her. All the while she remained hidden, we stood a chance of ... something. I didn't think Verity was going to come to our rescue, but maybe she would create a distraction. I just had to hope Rufus wouldn't bark.

Anna and Georgie were growling at him, their leads trapped under my foot as they strained forward.

Schooner dropped his gaze to them, and then the muzzle of his gun and my heart stopped again as I thought he was going to shoot my dogs.

'If they get out from under your foot, I'll shoot all your friends,' he threatened.

'You intend to kill them anyway,' I argued.

He inclined his head in agreement. 'Yes, but there are lots of ways to go.' Keeping the gun on us now that the four of us were all close together, he walked across the middle of the open space. 'Well done for finding the girl,' he chuckled. 'I hadn't realised she was nothing more than a housemaid. I don't think it matters now, of course.' In his left hand was the bag I'd seen him with at the bridge elevator. He placed it on the ground so he could operate the sea door controls.

It wasn't filled with weapons at all. 'That's the cash and jewels you took from Jack Langley, isn't it?'

'Yes,' he replied gamely. 'Well done again. Your friend the captain will force his way onto the bridge shortly. They'll get to the access hatch at the top, I would imagine, and find it to be already open.'

'You zip-lined down the wire, didn't you?' I tried to confirm. I knew he would have a plan to get down to the deck again without using the stairs or elevators. One option I considered was a parachute, but I wasn't convinced it had time to open. Another was the cable that ran from the rear of the bridge superstructure to the helipad about two hundred yards behind it. It was freezing out, but he didn't need to be exposed for very long. I had no idea what the wire's purpose was, I only knew it was there because I had seen them run banners out on it once or twice.

This time I got an impressed face to tell me I was right. 'You know, under different circumstances, you and I might have got on quite well, Patricia Fisher.'

I had an unpleasant retort for him but never got the chance because the sea door started to open and the cold swept in to steal my breath away. Molly, Barbie, and I were all soaked either fully or partially which meant we were already cold before the sub-zero temperatures hit us.

Just behind me, Sam was trying to do something. I could sense him moving one arm slowly, though I had no idea what he might be trying to do. I prayed he had a gun he'd picked up somewhere, even though I was certain that wouldn't be the case.

I glanced across to the other side of the room, flicking my eyes there and then back to Schooner. I still couldn't see Verity. Maybe, if he killed us, she would yet manage to stay hidden and survive. It wasn't an outcome I was ready to champion, I still wanted to get us all out of this.

'Are there really explosives on the ship? Barbie demanded to know.

Schooner chuckled, his shoulders shaking in amusement. I didn't think he was going to answer but he did. 'It doesn't matter either way, Miss Berkeley. We are on a collision course with a flow of ice bergs. The likelihood of this ship making it through is next to none. I admit, I shall be greatly disappointed, of course, if the Aurelia somehow survives, but I think it doubtful enough that I will make my exit now and watch the news tomorrow with interest. There is just one small matter of business to attend to before I go. I think it's time you all went for a swim.'

My teeth were already chattering from the cold, the danger of frostbite or other cold related injury becoming more likely by the second, but the thought of slipping into the water outside brought a whole new level of chill to my blood.

When none of us moved, he said, 'Or I can shoot you first and then toss you overboard. Yes,' he nodded to himself. 'I think that would be more fun.'

He raised his weapon meaningfully and time stood still for a heartbeat as Sam surged forward. He knocked me over, bumping my shoulder as he came from behind me with his right arm raised. He didn't have a gun, just a magnifying glass.

He threw it with all his might, aiming right for Schooner's head.

His throw was accurate, forcing Schooner to flinch his head right as he fired. The magnifying glass flew through the space where Schooner's head had been, out of the sea door, and into the freezing sea. The bullet caught Sam high on his left shoulder spinning him around as it slammed into his flesh.

Schooner's eyes were incredulous when I looked back up at him. 'What was that? Seriously? That's the best you can do? Even if it hit me, it wasn't going to stop your deaths.'

'It wasn't meant to stop you,' winced Sam, holding his shoulder as blood seeped through his fingers. 'It was meant to distract you.'

Schooner frowned. 'From what?'

'This,' said Verity and pulled the trigger on the spearfishing gun she held. The compressed air powered spear shot across the short distance just as Schooner turned his head to see who had spoken.

It hit him in the centre of his chest, impaling him instantly and carrying him out of the open sea door. I got the briefest glimpse of his shocked face, then he was swept from view and into the ocean. The cord connecting the spear to the gun went taut and snatched the gun from Verity's hands. She looked about ready to drop it anyway as she tried to juggle Rufus.

I fell to my knees to check on Sam. We were all in bad shape, all except Verity, but she'd just killed a man and now looked utterly wretched.

There hadn't been time to call or speak to anyone before, the need to see if I was right about Molly's location too pressing to wait, and Alistair's need to get the ship back under his control too important to bother him with the life of one person. Now though, we needed to get help, and we needed to get warm.

Barbie and Molly were suffering worse than me, neither had any bodyfat to insulate them, but we would all die of hypothermia if we didn't get out of our wet clothes soon.

The girls helped me get Sam to his feet. The poor man was going into shock from the pain of his injury. Together, taking my dogs, plus Rufus and Verity, we made our way out of the water sports centre and got the door closed. We were no warmer, but at least the icy chill from outside was no longer buffeting our bodies.

There was an elevator bank directly opposite the water sports centre so that passengers could find it easily. I staggered toward it, hoping my fingers could work the button even though I couldn't feel them. However, it bonged before I could get to it, the noise telling me the car had just arrived on our deck.

The doors opened to reveal a squad of armed security guards inside, and right at the front, holding an assault rifle in his hands, was Alistair.

I willingly collapsed into his arms.

Warming Up

Roughly twenty men and women spilled from the elevator. Among them was Jermaine, his sleeves rolled up to show his muscular forearms. He had an assault rifle just like Alistair's gripped in his hands. It looked out of place with his bow tie. Beside him was Agent Garrett, looking better than he did last time I saw him. I wondered if he had been looking for me and getting fretful for the last hour or more.

'Where is he?' begged Alistair.

'Dead,' I managed through my chattering teeth.

'Dead how?' His eyes betrayed how much he wanted to believe me.

Verity blurted. 'I shot him with a spear gun!' Attention swung her way just in time for everyone to see her faint. No one was close enough to stop her as she collapsed into a heap with Rufus landing on her chest where he'd been clutched in her arms. It all proved too much for her - stepping in to save us all at the last moment. When she pulled the trigger, her face had been a mask of calm. At the time, it made me wonder if she might be ex-forces or something; not so much now that she was white as a sheet and out cold on the deck. She and I would be sharing a drink when she felt better. Despite my earlier thoughts about not making friends, she was my age, came from my country, and we had things in common – like getting into insane and deadly capers on a cruise ship.

Two members of the crew scooped her from the deck and took her away, carrying her into the elevator while a third took Rufus's lead and went with them.

Hugging Alistair and probably making him cold rather than improving my own temperature, I said, 'I'd really like to warm up now. Are we still going to sink?'

'Not today,' he smiled down at me, holding me close and doing what he could to impart heat from his body. 'We have the bridge, and Commander Ochi has reset the ship's controls. It will take a while to undo all that Robert has done, but the ship is ours again, the danger has passed, and we are slowing down. It would appear there never were any explosives. I have teams down in the lowest sections of the ship now, and so far, they have found nothing. I'm glad to see you found your missing housemaid, but I think we should get you all to sickbay now. Especially this young man,' he was looking directly at Sam. 'He appears to have been shot.'

'I got shot!' cheered Sam, excitedly. 'Wait until I tell mum and dad!'

Though I felt like collapsing, I couldn't stop myself from laughing. It wasn't as if I could convince him to keep it a secret from his parents: he'd been shot. It's the sort of thing a parent will notice.

On unsteady legs, I let Alistair lead me into the elevator, but there I raised a hand to his chest to push him away. 'You have much to attend to. Jermaine can get me to sickbay.'

'It is my honour to do so, madam,' said Jermaine.

'I'm coming too,' insisted Wayne.

I met his eyes with mine, imparting kindliness, when I said, 'Please do, Agent Garrett. I shall feel so much safer with you beside me.' It wasn't necessarily true, but I knew he saved my life earlier today when Harry Tomlinson fired a wild shot. A memory forced its way to the front of my brain. 'Lieutenant Mashkov is working with Schooner,' I blurted through my cold blue lips. 'Molly, tell him.'

She didn't need to. Alistair put a hand on my arm to calm me. 'We found Mashkov's body already. It looks like Schooner shot him.'

I let my head loll forward. 'That's why he shot Tomlinson. Tomlinson was trying to surrender but Mashkov couldn't let that happen.'

'They were all in it together,' Alistair concluded.

I thought about his statement. 'They were pawns. That doesn't make them any less guilty, but they were just fools in a game where they didn't understand the rules. Or were lied to about the stakes.'

Alistair bowed his head. 'What a mess. Most of the passengers are unaware that anything has happened. A little well-placed PR and those who suspect something will be too busy drinking champagne to focus on it.'

'Do what you must for the passengers, Alistair.' I was trying to make it acceptable in his head. Then I spotted Molly and saw how cold she looked. Barbie wouldn't look much better. 'We really need to get to the sickbay and warm up.'

There was no argument from anyone, and the elevator doors closed, sealing the rest of the world outside. I breathed my first relaxed breath in hours and slumped against Jermaine as he held me close.

Breakfast

The following morning, I awoke to bright sunlight streaming through the windows of my bedroom. It was something I experienced almost every morning when I was on board for my three-month cruise around the world and it felt very homely.

By the side of my bed was a pitcher of water with a clean glass sat next to it. I rolled onto my back and stared at the ceiling, rerunning the previous day in my head. In the sickbay, with heated blankets on me, it still took ages before I felt warm again. Drs Kim and Davis insisted we drink warm beverages, a nurse supplying hot sweet tea and making us sip it continually.

The focus of attention wasn't on Sam, which surprised me. In the doctors' opinion, our condition was more critical. They, of course, stripped his shirt and jacket away to expose the wound, and gave him a shot of morphine even though he seemed to be enjoying himself.

By the time Melissa and Paul found him with the help of Lieutenants Bhukari and Baker, his wound was dressed, and he was singing something, a pop song I didn't know, over and over on loop. Melissa burst into tears, but she didn't blame me, or anyone else, the tears were just a by-product of overwhelming emotions. Dr Kim promised me Sam would be fine. He would suffer soreness and aches near the site of his wound – the bullet passed through his left deltoid – but no lasting ill-effects.

Alistair came to see me, arriving with a small entourage of guards. They looked both exhausted and wired at the same time. He felt a need to check on me, it made me feel cared for ... loved even. He was a tender man; I knew that for certain. He had dozens of things he needed to be doing but he came to check on me. The ship was safe again, that was the assurance he gave. Robert Schooner was gone. They didn't find his body, but how could they expect to? I saw the spear gun impale his chest before he fell into the frigid waves outside. I was content he would not come back this time.

When Alistair left, I fell asleep. Finally warm, fatigue and the exhaustion that follows constant adrenalin, drained my energy like water down a plughole. I didn't dream. I'm not sure I even moved in the two hours I was out.

Jermaine and Agent Garrett waited in the sickbay until we were all released and saw us safely back to our suite. It was nearly midnight by then, and I was hungry, but far too tired to consider doing anything other than going to bed.

Now it was morning and I felt like I could relax. Perhaps today I would finally get to have a massage and enjoy some of the benefits being on board a luxury cruise ship presented. I had a few items on my list of things to do today: check on Sam, take Verity for lunch and thank her for saving our lives, get a massage if I had time, but the most pressing was to check in with the person in cabin 34782.

It was a task I needed to perform alone, which meant I would have to slip away from Agent Garrett at some point. I felt bad about plotting to do so; just a few hours ago he dived in front of a bullet to save my life. Despite that, I still couldn't quite bring myself to let him into my inner circle. Where was he when we came back to the suite last night? He said he woke up from the painkiller induced slumber and went looking for me. I had no reason to doubt his words, no reason at all. Nevertheless, I needed to keep the person in cabin 34782 a secret from him and everyone else.

My chance came after breakfast. Agent Garrett went to the gym with Barbie, giving himself a break from watching me only because I promised to stay put. I didn't stay put of course, I gave them five minutes, waited until Jermaine went to his cabin for something, then grabbed the dogs and slipped out the door.

The dogs sniffed their way along as I made my way down to deck eight. When I stopped in front of cabin 34782, I didn't knock, not straight away. I checked left and right first, making doubly sure I was alone and only when I felt confident did I raise my knuckles to tap quietly on the door.

It opened to reveal a familiar face.

The End

Author's Note

Hi, there,

Thank you for reading my book. I hope you enjoyed it. Building up to putting Patricia and her friends back on the ship has taken a while; I wrote the first book in this series back at the very start of the year.

Today was touted to be the hottest day ever recorded in the UK. I didn't get to see the news to hear whether it was or not, but the temperature in the log cabin where I write was hot enough for me to choose to hide in the house instead. I have a stone floor in the kitchen which ensures it is always the coolest room in the house. There, I was able to edit and complete this story while still drinking copious amounts of water.

Tomorrow, I will be starting a new story, one starring Rex and Albert but it's not the next Rex and Albert book. I was invited by an author friend to submit a piece for a charity anthology. The charity is a hastily arranged enterprise to help a lady who is about to be ejected from her home. I don't know the lady, and I only met the author friend the one time, but it feels like a worthwhile thing to do. Plus, I get to create a secret Rex and Albert story which people will whisper about and try to find. It has to be a short story, which are so much harder to craft than a fifty-thousand-word novel because the action has to start on the first page, yet the characters still require introduction.

It is 2200hrs and my house is sweltering after heating up all day. The upstairs is even hotter; honestly, I might sleep in my son's paddling pool. It will cool down again soon, it is never this hot for very long, but I look forward to the rain returning because my garden is dry, parched, and brown. Autumn is right around the corner, but before the leaves begin to turn, I will have to let you know what happens with Patricia and the

Godmother. I already know, of course. It is something I am excited to share with you.

Take care.

Steve Higgs

June 2020

More Books with Patricia Fisher

Read the book that started it all.

A thirty-year-old priceless jewel theft and a man who really has been stabbed in the back. Can a 52-year-old, slightly plump housewife unravel the mystery in time to save herself from jail?

When housewife, Patricia, catches her husband in bed with her best friend, her reaction isn't to rant and yell. Instead, she calmly empties the bank accounts and boards the first cruise ship she sees in nearby Southampton.

There she meets the unfairly handsome captain and her appointed butler for the trip – that's what you get when the only room available is a royal suite! But with most of the money gone and sleeping off a gin-fuelled pity party for one, she wakes to find herself accused of murder; she was seen leaving the bar with the victim and her purse is in his cabin.

Certain that all she did last night was fall into bed, a race against time begins as she tries to work out what happened and clear her name. But the Deputy Captain, the man responsible for safety and security onboard, has confined her to her cabin and has no interest in her version of events. Worse yet, as she begins to dig into the dead man's past, she uncovers a secret - there's a giant stolen sapphire somewhere and people are prepared to kill to get their hands on it.

With only a Jamaican butler faking an English accent and a pretty gym instructor to help, she must piece together the clues and do it fast. Or when she gets off the ship in St Kitts, she'll be in cuffs!

More Cozy Mystery by Steve Higgs

Pork Pie Pandemonium

Baking. It can get a guy killed.

When a retired detective superintendent chooses to take a culinary tour of the British Isles, he hopes to find tasty treats and delicious bakes …

… what he finds is a clue to a crime in the ingredients for his pork pie.

His dog, Rex Harrison, an ex-police dog fired for having a bad attitude, cannot understand why the humans are struggling to solve the mystery.

He can already smell the answer – it's right before their noses.

He'll pitch in to help his human and the shop owner's teenage daughter as the trio set out to save the shop from closure. Is the rival pork pie shop across the street to blame? Or is there something far more sinister going on?

One thing is for sure, what started out as a bit of fun, is getting deadlier by the hour, and they'd better work out what the dog knows soon or it could be curtains for them all.

More Books by Steve Higgs

Blue Moon Investigations

Paranormal Nonsense

The Phantom of Barker Mill

Amanda Harper Paranormal Detective

The Klowns of Kent

Dead Pirates of Cawsand

In the Doodoo With Voodoo

The Witches of East Malling

Crop Circles, Cows and Crazy Aliens

Whispers in the Rigging

Bloodlust Blonde – a short story

Paws of the Yeti

Under a Blue Moon – A Paranormal Detective Origin Story

Night Work

Lord Hale's Monster

The Herne Bay Howlers

Undead Incorporated

Patricia Fisher Cruise Mysteries

The Missing Sapphire of Zangrabar

The Kidnapped Bride

The Director's Cut

The Couple in Cabin 2124

Doctor Death

Murder on the Dancefloor

Mission for the Maharaja

A Sleuth and her Dachshund in Athens

The Maltese Parrot

No Place Like Home

Patricia Fisher Mystery Adventures

What Sam Knew

Solstice Goat

Recipe for Murder

A Banshee and a Bookshop

Diamonds, Dinner Jackets, and Death

Frozen Vengeance

Albert Smith Culinary Capers

Pork Pie Pandemonium

Bakewell Tart Bludgeoning

Stilton Slaughter

Bedfordshire Clanger Calamity

Death of a Yorkshire Pudding

Free Books and More

Get sneak peaks, exclusive giveaways, behind the scenes content, and more. Plus, you'll be notified of Fan Pricing events when they occur and get exclusive offers from other authors because all UF writers are automatically friends.

Not only that, but you'll receive an exclusive FREE story staring Otto and Zachary and two free stories from the author's Blue Moon Investigations series.

Yes, please! Sign me up for lots of FREE stuff and bargains!

Want to follow me and keep up with what I am doing?

Facebook